In memory of my parents, Larry and Sherry, who gave
me a love for books

2

CHAPTER ONE

This was not the way she had imagined things. Lily recalled what Grandmother Winnie had told her on many occasions: "It's good to have dreams, but you let yours carry you too far". Not that her grandmother had discouraged her. She just knew that over fantasizing something only led to disappointment. So once again, here she was in the middle of an unpleasant shock.

She flicked her green eyes peevishly over the craft. The envisioned smooth, brightly painted wooden hull of the dirigible had morphed into a sad, faded, broken thing that mocked Lily, with its once great name still visible on the side. Told she could own history for only a modest sum of coin, she had jumped at the offer. After all, this was the great Robyn's Nest! Sir Robert Pettigrew had flown it himself during his famous adventures. She opened her bag and held up one of the posters that her grandmother had kept and shown her time and time again. Beautiful reds and yellows glowed from the ship and gave it a cheerful air while the bright blue balloons above lifted it into the sky. Memories of Sir Robert's stories told to her by candlelight at bedtime flashed through her mind. She had always dreamed of following in his footsteps. The fact that these adventures had happened 60 years prior to today's purchase had not reckoned into Lily's excited deliberations.

What was to be done? She had paid the man for it sight unseen because her visions of it had been so grand. She had found the advertisements posted up around town (without pictures she now realized!) and had decided this was finally her time to do something exciting and important. Lily had met the seller in his office by the shipyard, and he had given her the papers as he told her where it was parked on the landing strip. Lily had looked around the airfield at the newer, sleeker airships and then she noticed the wreck. She ran a hand through her dark hair and frowned. Could this piece of ancient history still fly? Oh, she wished she had not been so impulsive! She had used a good portion of the money her grandmother had left her when she had died the previous winter. Lily no longer had a comforter and protector to seek for advice. She tried not to panic. The only thing to be done was to go back to the man she had bought this travesty from and demand her money back.

When brought to it, Lily Annette Fairfax could be intimidating. She was taller than most girls her age, and her jet black hair and flashing cat-like green eyes lent her an air of mystery. People were not always sure what she would do. Even then, she was a jolly sort most of the time and many of her waking hours were spent daydreaming of adventure. Only 22 when her grandmother passed, she still lacked much of life's experience that would have made her more cunning and less gullible. She marched over to the office she had left only 30 minutes prior and knocked on the door. Silence answered her. She put her face against the small window and saw only a desk and chair. No lamps left burning, not a hint that anyone had even been there. She stopped one of the street cleaners who was just now passing over her current area of sidewalk with his broom.

"Do you know where the man that was in this office went? The seller who works for this shipyard?" she asked rather roughly, but not altogether unkindly.

"That man?" said the old, bent gentleman. "I saw him lock up a few moments ago as I rounded the corner."

He couldn't have gone too far in that time. Lily was determined to find him as soon as possible. She thanked the sweeper and headed off in the direction he had pointed out to her. Passing the airfield, she wound her way towards what she assumed was his destination: the Callingford train tracks. This was the ultimate destination where the road ended. She hurried past tall brick buildings that blocked the rising sun on her left, leaving a gloom on the road she was travelling. To her right were factories just opening for the day. The smoke rising from the chimneys mixed in with the morning mist, coming up to meet it from the cool ground.

As she arrived at the station, she took a quick glance around. There were people milling about everywhere. She kept her eye out for a short, puffy cheeked man with sharp eyes and protruding front teeth. It hadn't quite struck her before, but she realized he was quite rat-like, body and soul. A quick scurrying off to her right made her turn her head just in time to see said rodent rushing onto the train.

"Mr. Mallerson , return my money immediately!" she cried as she sped up the platform. Crowds of families bidding farewell and business men heading to the office blocked her way. Pushing through with quick apologies, she saw him sitting down by a window in a compartment further up the track. As she approached, he noticed her and gave a wide smile. He opened the window a crack and said "Why, Miss Fairfax, I thought you would be enjoying your purchase by now. What brings you here, with a crease in your brow?"

"You know perfectly well what brings me here! How dare you sell me something so run down and pass it off as the Robyn's Nest! I demand my money back at once!" She did not believe she could have been more emphatic.

Mr. Mallerson took on an expression of feigned hurt. "My dear lady, all sales are final. As I'm sure you could clearly see from the name on the side, it is indeed the famous Robyn's Nest. If you are not happy with its current state, what is that to me? I offered it, and you accepted. Now, if you don't mind..." With this he closed the window again.

Horrible man! she thought. She tried to make her way to the train steps only to hear the whistle and watch as it slowly pulled away. Here were all her hopes, dreams, and a decent amount of her money, departing on the morning train. She balled her hands into fists and screamed "You vermin-faced scoundrel!" at the departing car.

Beginning to get a few questioning looks in her direction, she left the train station and started to make her way back to the airfield. After inquiring of one of the guards, Lily learned that Mr. Mallerson had only recently rented that office and did not actually work for the airfield. Her heart thoroughly broken, she drug herself back to her recently acquired ruin. She placed her hand on the side and traced the letters. She sat down in the grass, hugged her knees and stared at the culmination of her dreams that lay in tatters. The whole thing was just too ridiculous! Poor Grandmother Winnie had tried to warn her against this very thing. She began to laugh at her silly self. And then she burst into tears.

Wiping her face and angry that she had let herself cry, Lily determined to look the Robyn's Nest over and see if there was any hope for it. The first thing she noticed was the broken boards that opened up spaces into the interior, where cobwebs hung in tatters.

The airships balloons were torn and threadbare. The aftmost ignition furnace was rusted and cracked. Famous though it once was, many people had forgotten Sir Robert Pettigrew and his machine, and it was left to rot. Only Lily had still held on to the hope that she could take it into the skies and start a new life. Her grandmother had meant everything to her and with her death Lily felt adrift. She figured she would take that feeling and literally go floating away, doing what she had always imagined as a child. Now she and the dirigible were land bound indefinitely.

Rising up off of the grass, she made her way over to a fringed rope ladder hanging off the deck. Eyeing it warily, she tugged on it to make sure it was secure and then made her way up. The boards up here creaked a bit but seemed sound enough. The airship was slightly tilted to the side from its last landing and walking across the deck was a bit of a challenge. Lily carefully stepped over to the stairs and looked down. The morning sun was filtering through the cracks in the side, making it not as gloomy as she had expected. Of course, no cracks would have been preferable. She put her hand on the wall to steady herself as she descended below deck.

She hadn't hoped that anything had been left of Sir Robert's voyages, especially after her initial disappointment of the exterior of the ship. However, painted on the side of the left wall was a vivid scene of palm trees and a still, quiet ocean. Lily ran her hands over it in awe. *"I know this place! Here is Zantislan!"*

Her favorite story from Grandmother Winnie's tales of Sir Robert was what she called "The Adventure of the Soundless Seas". The Robyn's Nest had lost an ignition furnace and Sir Robert had to land on an island with which he was unfamiliar. Being headed in the general direction of Capland, he had a good idea where he was, but this island was not on any of his maps. Landing in the sand, he decided to explore a little and see what was there. Once off the ship, he heard the crunch as his boots tracked through the sand and rocks on the beach and the chirp of birds in the nearby trees. The only thing he didn't hear was the sound of waves on the shore. He looked in surprise toward the ocean to see it sparkling like a mirror. It was still and quiet. Nothing like the other beaches he had seen with crashing waves and foam. He thought perhaps it was just due to a calm day and made his way into the trees on the interior of the island. Here, he found he was not alone. His disembarkation had been watched by a group of people who had hidden themselves behind the betel nut and palm trees. He noticed they wore wrapped fabric of dazzling colors and prints around their bodies and heads. Startled, he at first reached for his pistol, but after realizing they were unarmed he placed it back in his holster. Seeing he meant them no harm as well, they welcomed him to their village and to a meal. He became friendly with the inhabitants of the island while he completed his repairs, communicating through hand gestures. One day, they took him out to the beach and fitted him with a bamboo breather. They showed him the underwater mountain range encircling the island that kept the waters so strangely calm. He was astounded with all the plant and aquatic animal life found around these islands. Brightly colored, waving ferns greeted him. Multitudes of fish darted in and out of hidden caves. Some sort of seal-like creatures lounged on sandbars near the surface. Sir Robert had never seen anything like it. He always regarded this as the one true paradise of all his travels for the rest of his days. Rumors said after he retired he went back to stay.

Lily loved this story. She had always wanted to see the places he had been, but Zantislan most of all. Unfortunately, Sir Robyn had never kept any public maps of his discovery. He said he kept the location of it in his mind alone. He never wanted droves of people to find Zatislan and make it less than it was when he found it.

Looking ahead, she saw a desk affixed to the floor, the top worn shiny in places through years of use. She ran her hand lovingly over the surface. Sir Robert himself had sat at this desk! Here he had planned and dreamed. The chair he had used was long gone and the drawers were empty, but Lily was still enthralled. Behind her a window opened out into the dreary landing field. The sun continued to rise as the time crept closer to noon. A streak of light swept up the far wall where Lily could see a room tucked under the stairs in the far side of the ship. Crossing the decking, she opened the door to find a small room with an adjoining bathroom. No furniture was left of the bedroom but she could see where a hammock must have hung at one point. The bathroom wasn't large but it had enough room for a small tub that could be filled with hot water from a tiny boiler placed at the base with an adjoining water tank. They looked sound but a leak test would need to be performed at some point. That is, if anything could be made to work properly again. Walking over to the starboard side she checked the status of the storage room and kitchen. Empty, as she had well known. They were a decent size, though, and would hold enough goods for a long voyage. Lily sighed and climbed back up the stairs.

Now she moved on to inspect the burners. The one she had seen from below was indeed in sorry shape. A large gash crept up the right side of the pipe. The furnace itself was covered in rust. There was no way she could get this to work properly as it stood. The second furnace, while showing its age, was in much better shape. It was possible to fill the balloons with one furnace but it would not be easy. Her love of Sir Robert and his fantastic flying machine had led Lily to study steam mechanics for dirigibles when she had time to spend in the library. Unfortunately, reading something and actually physically fixing and flying something like this were two different things. She had a vague idea of what needed to be done but she was still at a loss as to how to begin. She walked over to the port side of the ship to look at the balloons that were draped haphazardly over the side. There was no saving them.

Lily walked home that afternoon with a dreary outlook on the world. Even the April sun shining down brightly on her through the breaks in the buildings couldn't improve her mood. How was she going to get everything she needed to fix the Robyn's Nest? Sure, she had a rudimentary understanding of how everything worked, but she needed new materials to get the ship sky-worthy again. Most of the money she had gotten from Grandmother Winnie was spent on that sad spectacle. What was left over would do for rent on their small apartment for another month, but she was going to have to find a different job or an even smaller apartment soon. While her grandmother was still alive, Lily had begun typing dictation from a local law firm. They mostly did small cases and the wages were not high, but it had been enough for her to chip in for living expenses along with her grandfather's pension that had helped keep them both going.

Reginald Fairfax, or Rex for short, was Lily's grandfather. He was a kind, hardworking man, strong as an ox but always willing to sit and play with Lily when he had time. After her mother had died from a fever when she was three and her father from an accident when she was 5, her Grandfather Rex and Grandmother

Winifred had taken her to raise in their son's stead. She only remembered lovely snippets of her mother, how she would hold her and sing to her. Her father she remembered more, with his soft, warm voice while he read to her and his big arms swinging her in the park on his days off. Her life with her grandparents had been wonderful. They were both warm, loving people, especially Grandmother Winnie. When Grandfather Rex died three years earlier, it had been from a long illness. Her Grandmother had passed from a cold that turned to pneumonia. She missed them all terribly and was glad she at least had a chance to say goodbye to her grandparents before they were gone. Now, she was all alone.

She opened the door of the apartment building and climbed the stairs to her flat on the third floor. She entered, hung her coat by the door, and sat dejectedly on the chair by the window. The phrase 'buy in haste, repent in leisure' flashed through her mind. How could she have wasted her grandmother's inheritance so easily? At the time, it seemed like the most reasonable purchase. Chasing dreams always feels that way. To let your head float in the clouds is fine, but one foot always has to be planted firmly on the ground. Lily felt like she had been having a hard time making decisions recently. Nothing felt right anymore. Any time she had problems in the past, Grandmother Winnie would make her tea and sit down and talk with her. That's what she needed; tea.

Lily got up and moved to the kitchen. The tea box was almost empty, matching the bare cupboard it sat within. She put the water on to boil and took stock of what was left in the pantry. A few cans left of odds and ends but nothing left in the icebox. These would have to last to the end of the week. As the teapot started to whistle, Lily thought she heard something by the front entrance. She removed the pot to the counter and then went to the door. Then she heard a distinct knock. She opened it to find a small, wizened old man standing in the hallway.

"I'm so sorry to bother you Miss Fairfax, but I'd like to speak with you if you have a moment. I got your name and address from the log at the airfield. I know it's very presumptuous of me, but it's about the Robyn's Nest," wheezed the old gentleman. He seemed rather out of breath. Lily looked him over, or really looked down upon him as he was only about five and a half feet high. His white hair puffed out of his head on either side and his clothes were slightly rumpled. Still, he had a kind face and certainly seemed friendly. Lily felt he was not a threat and invited him inside.

She offered him tea and he gladly accepted. "I feel awfully bad showing up like this unannounced. My name is Collin Applegate. When I heard that upstart Mr. Mallerson had bought the Robyn's Nest through underhanded dealings my heart sank. I tried to persuade him to let me have it, but he refused to take the amount it was actually worth. I'm sorry to say he then found you as a willing buyer."

Lily groaned. "The whole ordeal has been rather embarrassing for me as you can imagine, Mr. Applegate. What I don't understand is what your interest is in that wreck, wonderful and fascinating as it is. Honestly, though, I don't care. If you want to buy it off of me I'm quite willing. I think I've learned that planting all your hopes on a dream only gives you mud in the end. I've given up."

"Oh, no! Oh no, don't do that, please. Aspirations are wonderful things to have. You just need to temper them with wisdom. Please don't frown; I'm sorry if I've offended you. The excitement of youth is a wonderful thing. When you get as old as I am you sometimes forget what it feels like. However, there are people who will take advantage of it, as you well know. I would like to help you Miss Fairfax. You see, my father used to be Sir Robert's mechanic, and I learned the business by helping him."

Lily furrowed her brow slightly. She had always thought that Sir Robert had done all his work alone. None of the stories had ever mentioned a helper.

"I know what you're thinking. The writers and reporters were only interested in his adventures and fantastic feats. Nobody cared who did maintenance for his ship when he was in port." Mr. Applegate gave a small chuckle. "Honestly, that suited my father and me just fine. We didn't want to mess about with any of those people. They rarely left the poor man alone."

Lily nodded. She could see how that wound put a damper on things. "But whatever can be done now? You've seen the sorry state the airship is in. I certainly don't have the funds to fix it. I barely make enough to buy necessities and I still need to find a way to keep my apartment. I'm afraid that I am just going to have to take my losses here."

Mr. Applegate slowly nodded his head. "Yes, you could do that. But what if you could fix it?"

Lily thought for a moment. "I would love to fix it. It's everything I've dreamed of doing. It just isn't possible."

A smile broke over Mr. Applegate's face. "I have wanted to fix up the old Robyn's Nest for a long time. When Sir Robyn retired from his adventures, he wanted to leave the Robyn's Nest here so no one would come looking for it, or him. It was meant to be left to my father, but the trustees of his estate claimed they couldn't find the final signed will and with no living relatives, they sold it off to the highest bidder. It's been going around from buyer to buyer until it ended up with this Mr. Mallerson that has given you so much trouble. "

"If you're interested," he continued, "I would like to offer you a job that would entail helping my wife

16

around the house and assisting me with rebuilding the airship. We can offer you room and board. My wife, Hannah, has trouble getting around and would love the extra hand. She has already agreed, so I just await your decision." Mr. Applegate looked at Lily with expectation.

Lily was overwhelmed. She waited so long to reply that Mr. Applegate began to look nervous. "Your kindness is overwhelming, sir," she said quietly. "I happily accept".

"Bother my kindness!" said Mr. Applegate, laughing. "I only want another go at getting the Robyn's Nest back in working order! I've been retired long enough. And don't worry. I have no designs on it if you wish to keep it. It belongs in the hands of someone with big dreams and the youth to follow them. Now, if you would be so obliged, Hannah and I would love to have you to dinner this evening to work out the details. Here's the address. We'll see you around 6:30."

She smiled and nodded as Mr. Applegate, or Collin as he insisted, handed her a slip of paper with an address written upon it. And with that, he shook her hand and left.

After the door closed, Lily absently wandered to the sofa and rather fell more than sat down into it. *What a day! I have gone from one extreme to the other. I don't quite know what to think of it all. I'm glad he gave me some time to recover.* Lily glanced at the clock. *I have about 3 hours to compose myself before the Applegates expect me for dinner.*

Getting up from the sofa, Lily began to put the tea things away. "I suppose," she said aloud, "that this means I will be leaving the apartment." She knew this was a silly thing to say, because she had already known that she would have to leave sooner or later since she could no longer afford to live there. A melancholy mood came over her. This was where all her memories were. She began to wander the flat and stopped in each room. This stove was where Grandmother Winnie had taught her to cook. Her bedroom was the background for all the adventure stories Lily loved. Tears came to her eyes, and she began to furiously wipe them away.

After Lily had reminisced and the kitchen was cleaned, Lily went to change for dinner. She only had one "good" dress that was horribly old but would have to do for this evening. She pulled her hair up into a knot and donned a pair of her grandmother's earrings as well. The spring evenings were still chilly so she grabbed her coat as she headed out the door.

Following the directions that Collin has given her, Lily noticed he lived quite close to the airfield, which made sense considering his recent occupation there. As she passed by the yard, she could just see the

18

edge of the Robyn's Nest. She sighed. "I hope Collin is right about this."

Finally arriving at the Applegate's home, Lilly knocked on the door. A light shone through the glass side panel onto the dark road, imbuing it with a cheery warmth. Lily wasn't sure what to expect in this new adventure, but she began to have hope.

CHAPTER TWO

Mrs. Hannah Applegate opened the door with a rosy-cheeked smile and invited Lily inside. For a woman who allegedly had a difficult time getting around, she certainly moved quickly and gracefully enough. She took Lily's hat and coat and placed them on the rack in the entryway.

"Welcome, my dear!" she said brightly and motioned for Lily to follow her inside. The house was small, but cozy and orderly. Lily wondered to herself what exactly it was that she was supposed to help with here.

"You have a lovely home," said Lily. "I must say, I was under the impression that you had a hard time keeping up with the house chores." She couldn't seem to stop herself from asking, and hoped that it hadn't been rude.

"Oh goodness, Collin is always worrying over me. I do have occasional back issues that lay me up from time to time that have been getting more frequent. I'm not someone who can't ask for help though and I'm thrilled to have an assistant." Here Hannah gave Lily another one of her warm smiles and this put her at ease.

Hannah escorted her into the living room and offered her a seat. Collin was already there smoking a pipe, which Hannah looked askance at but said nothing. "I'll just be a moment. You sit here and talk with Collin for a bit. I have a few more dinner preparations to finish and then we can move to the dining room." With this Hannah left through a door to the right, toward what Lily assumed was the kitchen.

Lily sat down on a soft, flower printed couch near Collin and looked around the room. It was small and homey, with a fire on the right hand side and a merrily ticking grandfather clock in the corner. She had faint memories of something like this in the house she lived in with her parents before their passing. Everything was a bit hazy from that time, but the remembrance of it gave her a warm, safe feeling that helped calm her anxiety. A beautiful, fluffy cat with orange and white fur jumped up on her lap and began purring as she pet it. This truly seemed like a wonderful home.

"Sorry. Duchess likes to greet guests to our house. I hope you don't mind. You won't be a guest for long though, I suppose! You can think of this as your home, too"

Smiling, Lily said "I think she's lovely. And thank you. It's been a while since I have felt home anywhere away from my grandparents."

"We'll get you settled down here in no time. I won't lie to you, though. I'm terribly excited to get to work on the old ship. The Robyn's Nest will be right as rain in no time."

At this point, Hannah popped her head back in the room and called them in to dinner. Lilly followed them into a small but well decorated dining room with a table full of wonderful looking dishes. It had been a while since Lily had eaten so well. Between her job and only having herself to cook for, she had certainly not had any opportunity or inclination to make anything elaborate at home. "This looks wonderful!" she said. "Thank you again for your kindness."

Hannah beamed. "Oh goodness, this is nothing at all! We're so happy you're here. If there's anything you're particularly interested in, I can even teach you to cook it while you're here." Lily gladly nodded her assent.

Dinner soon flew by filled with roast chicken, sausage stuffed potatoes, fresh asparagus, and lively chatter. When dessert was brought, Lily was almost too full to eat it, but would never pass on apple dumplings. She gave a contented sigh after laying her spoon down.

"Well, my dear, "said Collin. "What do you say? Is everything to your liking? We can have you moved in here within the week. We have an extra bedroom that Hannah has just aired out and is ready for any furniture you would like to bring. We can store anything else that may not fit."

"Now, Collin, don't be rushing her out of her home! She may not be ready quite yet," begged Hannah.

"No..," Lily began, "I am ready. I think I've been ready for some time to start something new."

Collin winked at his wife. "Just as I suspected. I'd be happy to come by late tomorrow morning and start helping you get things together at the apartment. Shall we say 10am?"

Lily nodded and shook Collin's hand. She then helped Hannah bring the dishes into the kitchen and lent a hand as they were cleaned and put away. Mrs. Applegate was efficient and organized and it made the task go by quickly. Collin was busy stoking the fire when they came back into the living room. "Nice and warm!" he said. "Duchess insists on being comfortable during her naps," he noted as he pointed toward the sleeping cat on the chair nearest the fireplace.

The grandfather clock began to chime nine o'clock and Lily started to say her goodbyes. Collin said he would walk her back home after making sure Hannah was comfortable in her chair. "I'll be but a moment, dear," he said as he kissed her on the head.

Hannah replied "You both be careful. The sidewalk is uneven out that way. I hope you had a nice evening, Lily, and I look forward to having you here. Good night!"

Lily thanked Hannah profusely once again, and then she and Mr. Applegate headed back toward the apartment building.

"What a wonderful time! It's been too long since we've had a young person to add energy to our conversations. Our son, Thomas, lives out of town and we sadly don't get to see him very often. I think this will be a perfect arrangement for all of us. Certainly livens things up!"

Laughing, Lily replied "I hope so! I'm looking forward to it myself. Does your son live very far away?"

Collin sighed a little. "He was never interested in taking over the mechanic business from me. He has an uncle that gave him an apprenticeship in his law office in Darvenshire, about 5 hours away by train. He really isn't a bad sort of man; he just has too much business on the brain. We generally see him and his wife and the grandchildren during Christmastime. "

Lily nodded. "I see. That must be hard not seeing them more often."

"It can be," he acknowledged. "Christine, his wife, writes us about the children quite often, so we have that. She's a very caring woman. I think she wishes they lived a little closer as well."

They arrived at Lily's apartment and bid each other good evening. Collin promised to be back around 10 the next morning to help her start moving her belongings.

When Lily entered her rooms, she still had a wash of nostalgia, but this time it was not as sad. She was beginning to see life from a new direction, and this gave her hope. She began to pack up a few odds and ends and then went to bed, full of expectations of the next morning.

Early the next day, Lily was up and making good progress in her packing. She had found some old crates behind the apartment and was filling them with all her worldly goods, which were not many. The tea table and chairs and the grandfather clock were the only large furniture pieces that belonged to her; the only bed she had left belonged to the apartment building. Any other furniture had been sold when her grandmother had died. She hoped she would be able to keep these few things with Collin's blessing. Everything else was silverware, dishes, and clothes, along with her grandmother's ring she always wore, and her grandfather's that she kept in a box.

With these small things packed away, not much was left to do when Collin arrived, except to load them onto the cart that he had brought. Lily had informed the landlord the night before that she would be moving, so nothing impeded their start to her new home. She hopped up beside him in the front of the cart as Collin directed the horse. She gave one more glance back toward her old life with a bittersweet smile.

When they arrived at the Applegate house, Hannah met them at the door and supervised the unloading of the cart. Lily's table, chairs, and clock were able to be moved into her new room, and any odds and ends that she didn't need right away were taken to the cellar.

After this was finished, Lily helped Hannah put together a quick lunch and they all sat down to relax for a moment.

After the meal, Collin leaned back in his chair and said "Let's go on over to the Robyn's Nest and start a preliminary list of items we need to repair". Lily assented and after helping Hannah put dishes away, they headed over to the yard.

"Most things are never as bad as they look on first glance," Colin said reassuringly. "And what is broken can almost always be fixed or replaced."

Lily smiled at his kind words. She knew he wanted as badly as she did to get the Robyn's Nest back in the air.

The spring sun was beginning to warm up the air, making the walk pleasant. Arriving at the yard, they checked in with the overseer to let him know they would begin working on the airship soon, and headed over to make notes of the damage.

Collin took out his clipboard and began to write while taking inventory aloud. "New balloons needed. Pick up some boards to fix the holes in the side." He climbed the ladder to the deck. "With some reinforcement, this furnace should be fine, but the other one needs replaced." After checking the interior, he also pronounced that a new, small boiler for the bathtub would also be needed.

"See? This really isn't too bad. This old girl was just left to sit for far too long and not properly taken care of. The balloons shouldn't be a problem; I'm fairly sure I have some in my workshop. The furnace and boiler we will have to hunt down. Now, let's head over to the lumber yard and pick up the boards."

They headed back to the Applegate's house to pick up the wagon and then made their way to the lumber yard. The sweet smell of freshly cut wood met them at the entrance. Lily had never been near the yard before and was amazed at the stacks upon stacks of boards in all different shapes and sizes. Collin wandered over to a group of cedar planks and began to take measurements. "We'll need about eight of these, four yards long," he said, mostly to himself.

After they made their purchase, the two loaded up the planks into the wagon and went back to Collin's workshop. "Let's check the workshop and make sure I still have those extra balloons. We'll wait for tomorrow to start hunting down a furnace."

Back at the house, Lily followed Collin over to his workshop. This was her first time entering this area of the house, and she was impressed by how clean and organized it was. "This is where I kept everything needed to fix the Robyn's Nest back in its heyday." Collin said. "Of course, I haven't had a need to keep things around since it's been years following Sir Robert's retirement. I'm technically retired, but I still do small repairs for the town now."

Digging through some crates in the back, Collin brought out a periwinkle blue mass of fabric. "Here we are! Let's check them for holes." Carefully, Collin and Lily laid out the balloons in the side yard and checked over each section. "I bought these a few years ago, hoping that I would have a chance to use them to repair the Robyn's Nest. When she was sold out of my control, I thought I would never have an opportunity to get them back out. I'm glad I kept them! They aren't the newest ones on the market, but they're in good shape and have been kept out of the elements."

"They're beautiful. Just like I imagined they would be. Do you really think we can get everything back the way it was?

"Or better! Or at least working," laughed Collin.

They carefully rolled the balloons back up and placed them safely away. After helping Collin put a few boxes back, Lily went back inside the house to see what she could do to help Hannah with dinner.

Hannah met her at the door with a broad smile. "Collin hasn't been this happy in years. This has really perked him up. He just moped around the house and got in my way when he wasn't working on a job," Hannah chortled.

"I'm glad I can be some sort of help after all this. I can't tell you how thankful I am to both of you for your assistance."

"Oh goodness, we're happy to have you! I'm sure Collin told you about our son and how little we see the family. It's nice to have a young person around."

After dinner was made, eaten, and cleared away, everyone made themselves comfortable in the living room. Duchess even deigned to let Lily pet her as she purred next to her on the sofa. Collin stretched out on his chair and ottoman by the fire while Hannah began on her sock knitting.

"It's been so long since I have been able to sit and relax," said Lily. "I had almost forgotten what it feels like".

Collin chuckled and began to light his pipe before catching a disdaining glance from Hannah, and then quickly thought better of it. "How many tales of Sir Robert and the Robyn's nest are you familiar with, Lily?" he asked instead.

"Oh, Grandmother Winnie would always tell me his stories before I went to sleep as a child. My favorite is Zantislan, but I love all of the ones I heard," Lily replied.

"There are quite a few...but still more that were never written up in the papers. For instance, have you ever heard about the time he met the speechless tribe in Yurisvenia?" he queried.

Lily shook her head no.

"Sir Robert had landed in Allegande to pick up supplies. In the marketplace he noticed a uniquely dressed group of people signing to a tradesman, who evidently understood, and prepared the items they needed. On further inquiry, he learned that they lived about two days away in Yurisvenia and came into town now and again for supplies. None of them spoke, even to each other, and only used their own kind of sign language to communicate. The trades people of the village had picked up enough to understand what they needed, and they all seemed to get along well enough. Sir Robert was intrigued, and decided to try and ask the group if he could come with them to the village and see how they lived. After a few failed gestures, they finally understood he wanted to join them and welcomed him along. He left the Robyn's Nest in the local airfield and only carried his travel bag to walk through the mountain path. He had never been with a group of people that remained in silence for so long. As it was, he himself was afraid to break the stillness by his own voice, knowing no other would join him. He knew the Yurisvenians could hear, because they would point out different birds as they listened to their songs along the trail. They tried to sign to Sir Robert what they were, but he could not understand. They stopped that evening in a small glade near the top of the mountain to rest. They all quietly fixed a small meal and sat down to eat. Afterward, they sat around the fire and watched as an older man was telling a story, or at least that was what Sir Robert thought he was seeing. In the morning, they began their journey again and came to their village about midday. Some people looked warily at the stranger the group had brought, but most people nodded at him in welcome. The older gentleman that was the storyteller of the night before took him to his house and showed him where he could sleep. Sir Robert was introduced to the man's wife as well as his son and the son's family. That evening, there was a celebration to welcome their guest. Sir Robert was amazed to find that while the occupants of the village were mute, they were quite skilled musicians. While they could not express themselves in speech, they were quite eloquent and emotive while using many instruments: Sir Robert saw stringed and wind instruments of kinds he had never known before. Drums of multiple sizes accompanied them. This performance was better than some symphony orchestras he had seen at home in Callingford, and theirs were lauded all over the world. There was dancing and a feast long into the night. Sir Robert went to bed happier than he had been in a long time. He decided to stay for a month and learn their sign language and culture. He always spoke quite highly of the Yurisvenians, but the newspaper men said the story wasn't 'flashy' enough."

Lily was enthralled. It was almost like being a small girl at bedtime again. She longed to go and meet all kinds of different people and travel the world. She hoped she would soon get her wish.

"There's one more thing I should tell you. Did you ever wonder why the Robyn's Nest was still here, when Sir Robert had retired in Zantislan?"

Lilly shook her head. "I guess I had never really thought about it."

"He had me sail with him that last flight. We traveled far south, at least 8 days past Allegande, until he brought the ship down and I could see the island in the water. It was in the middle of nowhere, far off the regular air routes. Having already made friends with the Zantislantians, they greeted us on the beach when they saw the Robyn's Nest land. We said our final goodbyes, and he told me to head north until Allegande and then make my way home. I came out a bit further east and had to re-direct the ship, so I can't tell you exactly where it is, but I can try to mark it as best as I can on a map for you."

"Oh, Collin! That would be wonderful! It's the one place I would like to see more than all the others."

The fire began to burn down and Lily wished the Applegates goodnight before heading to bed in her new room. She lay there for a while in the dark, thinking of all the things that had happened recently. She was so thankful for her new friends and excited to start work on the Robyn's Nest. She finally drifted to sleep, dreaming of exciting, uncharted lands.

CHAPTER THREE

A rooster began to crow, which startled Lily awake. At first, she didn't know where she was. Then she remembered the past few days and her new living situation. She breathed a sigh of relief. She still had the small pit of sadness in her stomach when she awoke, remembering her grandmother was no longer there, but this was a dull ache compared to how it was when her grandmother had first died. She still missed her terribly. She was glad to be in friendly company now, though, and got up to greet the day and help with breakfast.

She quickly went through her morning ablutions and got dressed. Making her way downstairs, she saw that Hannah had just started the fire in the living room and was happily humming away in the kitchen. Lily joined her and helped put some rolls in the oven as Hannah fried huge slabs of bacon.

"I haven't eaten like this in years! I'm going to be in danger of outgrowing my clothes if I'm not careful," she joked.

"You'll be fine," laughed Hannah. "You'll be far too busy working on that airship to gain any weight."

Lily couldn't wait to get started. She knew Collin was taking her out to look for a new furnace and boiler today. After they ate, Collin grabbed the wagon and they headed into town.

They arrived at the merchant just as he was opening for the day. They found a boiler for the tub in short order, but there was no ignition furnace that would work for the old ship. After some negotiations, Collin managed to get a deal on one from a catalog that the merchant could have in stock in a month or so. Lily was disappointed to hear how long it was going to take to get one in, but Collin said it would give them time to get everything else in order first.

"Collin, I don't know how I am going to be able to repay you for all of this. I still have my typing job here and there when they send me things, but it doesn't bring in much. I can give you all I have to help pay for the restoration, but I don't know how much this will cost."

"Good gracious!" exclaimed Collin. "You don't think I expected you to pay for all of this yourself, do you? No, that's my fault for not being clear. I don't want you to worry about paying for any of this. You own the ship, it's yours. But I feel like it's my responsibility to get it airborne again. It has been my life's work and I don't intend to shift it to anyone else, not yet anyway. All I need from you is your help to get the work done."

"I can never thank you enough for all of your help. You're a good man, Collin."

Collin blushed. "Well now...I don't know about that. I'm just doing what anyone would. It's just craftsman's pride, that's all," he said, embarrassed.

Lily smiled.

"At any rate, let's go back and get the boards and we can start cutting sizes for the ship" he said.

After a quick stop at the house to pick up the supplies and a lunch basked that Hannah had made for them, they headed to the shipyard. Lily wasn't an experienced carpenter, but she was determined to learn everything she needed in order to rebuild this airship. Collin was a patient teacher, and together they made good progress on their first day of repairs. They came back tired, but happy with their work.

That night, after dinner, Collin brought up an issue that had been bothering him.

"Lily, I don't want to frighten you, but I'm worried about you going out on adventures and having no way to protect or provide for yourself. Would you be willing to take some pistol lessons?"

Lily thought about this. "I can't say it hasn't crossed my mind before. I would hate to have to kill anyone, but I understand that it would be shear foolishness not to have some kind of protection. I don't even know how to hunt for that matter."

"Well, I just happen to know of a great teacher. And no, I don't mean myself. I'm a builder, not a marksman. But Hannah here," Collin gestured to his wife, "she has won multiple sharp shooting contests. She used to travel in a show when she was younger. It's how we met, actually."

Hannah grinned. "Collin was a volunteer from the audience. He was terrified, but never actually in danger. After I shot the apple off of his hat, he asked me on a date. We've been in love ever since."

Lily was in shock. This petite woman was a gun slinger? "Your back," Lily stuttered "I thought you had back trouble."

"Oh, I do from time to time. It's from all the tricks I used to do. Firing from horseback, shooting upside down from a trapeze...it certainly has caught up with me. I still have plenty of energy though and I still practice to keep my aim good."

Head still in a whirl, Lily nodded her agreement to being taught the basics. She still had a lot to learn about the Applegates.

"If I may borrow her tomorrow morning, Collin, we can have our first lesson. You can do your ship work in the afternoon."

And that was that. The next morning, Lily followed Hannah out to a field with an old, dilapidated barn. Hannah put up a target on the weathered boards and had Lily aim at it and fire. She didn't even hit the barn. Hannah laughed, and then stopped herself. "I'm sorry. The saying, you know. Don't worry. This is your first time even holding a gun. You will get this." Lily laughed, too, and kept trying. Her fifth shot hit the side of the target.

"There you go," called Hannah. "Keep your eyes open and your arms straight."

By the time they went home for lunch, Lily had hit the target once more on the very edge, which Hannah declared was a good first day.

"We're not in a rush, dear. The most important thing is that you are comfortable handling the pistol and won't hurt yourself or anyone else accidentally."

"I've never had to shoot anything in my life. I understand the necessity, I just don't know if I would be able to hunt anything."

"Believe me dear. If you get into a scrap and need protein, you will be happy to find a rabbit to shoot. Hopefully it won't come to that, but better to be prepared."

Back to the yard that afternoon, Lily and Collin got half of the boards up on the side of the ship. Things were starting to look up.

Over the next few weeks, Lily had pistol lessons with Hannah in the mornings and then helped build the Robyn's Nest in the afternoons. Both began to improve incrementally, though Lily knew she was still not hitting the target as much as Hannah would like.

Collin soon received word that the ignition furnace had come in to the store. He and Lily took the wagon out to pick up the furnace the next day. Everything else on the Robyn's Nest had been completed: the sides were newly patched, the boiler was installed, and the balloons were attached. They had even added new, bright coats of paint to make the old ship look like herself again. This was the last piece. The pair acknowledged the importance of this on their drive to the yard to install it.

"Are you ready for this?" Collin asked as they turned into the airfield.

Lily nodded. "Yes. I can't believe how far everything has come. Once again, I cannot thank you enough for your help."

"Don't thank me until we take her up and you see how she steers!" Collin laughed.

Collin waived to a few of the crew working around the shipyard to have them help them haul up the new furnace and Lily helped guide it into place. That afternoon was spent affixing it to the ship and teaching Lily the basic mechanics. She had seen plenty of diagrams and knew mostly how it worked, but actually having one in front of her helped to make sense of the writings.

"Well...shall we take her up?"

Taking a deep breath, Lily said "Yes. I think I'm ready".

The two ignited the furnaces, and the balloons began to inflate. Even with their enormous size, the balloons took less than an hour to be ready. Collin released the lines holding the ship in place and they began to slowly rise. Collin helped Lily steer over the yard and across to the nearby bay to get some room to fly. Lily took the ship up and around the area, thrilling to look down on all the boats in the water below. This felt like freedom. As the sun began to set, Collin helped Lily to bring the ship back around to the airfield and land it in its zone. With a small pang in her chest, the only thorn in the rose of this day, was Lily's wish that Grandmother Winnie could have seen her.

CHAPTER FOUR

Things really began to bustle at the Applegate's home after Lily's maiden voyage. April turned into May, then early June. Her airship lessons improved a great deal. She could use the stars for direction, find places on her map, and make near perfect landings. Her pistol lessons, however, were not improving as easily.

Lily bemoaned this fact to Hannah. "I just can't seem to hit the target most times. I'm trying to follow your instructions, but nothing seems to work for me. Maybe I just don't have the eye for this."

"Nonsense! Most people aren't born with perfect talents, you have to culture them. And even if you don't think you have any talent with a pistol, practicing will improve your aim. You just have to find out what works for you."

All the rest of June and into July, Lily practiced with the pistol from early morning late into the night. Some days she felt like she was making progress and hitting the target more, and other days it seemed hopeless. One morning while she was out at the barn again, she remembered something her Grandmother Winnie had told her. "You need to stop stressing so much about making things perfect. You can pour your whole heart and soul into something and exhaust yourself, and still not be happy with the results. You need to learn to relax, and enjoy what you're doing. You can still be happy knowing you did your best, and not worry if the outcome is perfect."

Lily took a deep breath, aimed her pistol, and hit the bullseye. She gaped for a minute, not sure if she was seeing things correctly. Hannah had just been coming to check on her and saw the whole thing. She came up clapping and said "Ah, you finally found what helps you. Congratulations!"

After this accomplishment, Lily could hit the target more regularly, even if she didn't hit the bullseye every time. Hannah upgraded her to bottles she tied onto a string to give her more of a challenge. She would set them swaying, which drove Lily crazy, but she still managed to hit them more often than not.

At this point, Lily's competence in the pistol and the airship had increased to the point that both Collin and Hannah felt comfortable Lily could handle things on her own.

One evening at dinner, Collin looked at Lily and said "Just remember. You don't have to go until you are ready. You don't have to go at all if you don't feel prepared. No one is forcing you out."

Lily smiled at his kindness. "I know. I want to go. I have dreamed my whole life of traveling the world in the Robyn's Nest. How many people get to live their dreams? I can't stop now."

Collin chucked. "I thought you might say that."

The plan was made for Lily to begin her journey at the beginning of August. Preparations were made for provisions and various odds and ends she would need to stay comfortable while she travelled. Lily provided as much of these for herself as she could with her small income, but she knew this would be gone as soon as she left. She would have to be able to fend for herself out in the world. The Applegate's gave Lily what she would allow them to offer, under protest, since she already felt that she owed them a huge debt of gratitude already. They were some of the kindest people she had ever met. She by no means wanted to take advantage of them, but trying to stop them from helping was like trying to reign in a whirlwind.

The cock crowed and the sun rose cheerfully on the day of her departure. Lily rose as well with a song in her heart and only a gentle ache. She packed the rest of her things in her carpet bag and went out to the kitchen for one final breakfast with the Applegates.

Hannah hugged her, crying. "I'll miss you so much! Don't ever hesitate to come back and visit. This is your home for as long as you want it. Remember what Collin taught you about mapping the stars. You'll always know where we are. Feel free to send us a note here and there if you have the opportunity. We'd love to hear from you."

"I won't forget. And thank you. This has truly felt like a second home to me. You've been so kind. I will try to write, and you'll be the first to know all my stories when I return." Lily gave Hannah a squeeze.

Collin had the wagon ready to carry Lily and the rest of her belongings to the Robyn's Nest. Both were lost in thought and didn't speak much on the drive over. Finally Collin said "I'm proud of you, Lily."

This took Lily by surprise, and she had to compose herself for a moment. "Thank you, Collin. I didn't know if I would ever hear someone say that to me again. God bless you for all your help and concern. You know I couldn't have done this without you and Hannah. If there is anything I can ever do for the both of you, please don't hesitate to ask."

"All Hannah and I want is to see you safe and happy, and to watch the Robyn's Nest soar the skies again. It has been too long since she has had a good adventure. Make sure she gets to see the world again."

"I will. At least, I will do my best."

"That's all any of us can do, my girl," Collin added, smiling.

At the yard, Collin and Lily loaded the ship and did a final check of all the systems and cargo. Lily was set for about three months with canned food stores. Hannah had given her a few fresh fruits and vegetables, but any other produce she would have to pick up along the way. Collin gave her a map of Sir Robert's favorite shopping areas in each city he would frequent when he needed supplies. He wasn't sure how many of these were still around, but it gave Lily a start.

"Remember, only fly at night when you have clear skies, and don't fly in thunderstorms. There are huge storms that can blow up out of nowhere during the late fall, so make sure you find a good place to settle while they blow over," Collin warned.

"I know, Collin, I'll be careful"

"Do you have enough coins? Remember, some areas only do straight trades and don't use any currency. Make sure you have things to bargain with in those cases."

"I know, Collin. Hannah gave me 5 huge sacks of sugar and some seeds just for that purpose."

"Hannah gave you plenty of ammo and powder for your pistol, too, right?"

"Yes, Collin. She set me up with tons." Lily laughed.

"I'm sorry; you know I can't help but worry about you. I just want to make sure you are as set as you can be, at least with anything we can help with." Collin sighed.

Lily gave Collin a big hug. "I know. And I appreciate it. I've never done anything like this and I'm worried enough myself. You have given me more than I ever dreamed to be possible. Now I just have to go and do it."

After inflating the balloons and finishing their goodbyes, Collin climbed down the rope ladder on the side of the ship and released the anchor rope for Lily. She called a last goodbye from the deck. He waved as he watched her sail into the skies and head south, towards lands known and otherwise.

CHAPTER FIVE

Lily waved at Collin as he watched her from the ground and set her course. She truly wanted to find Zantislan, but she only knew it was located somewhere to the south, where Collin had made his best guess. It was quite a distance to Allegande, so Lily decided to find some of the nearer places from Sir Robert's adventures as she made her way down.

Looking at her map, Lily noticed she was heading toward the Forest of Avoclaide. Sir Robert had been there after a great fire. There was a village that had been comprised of connecting buildings built into the treetops, and the conflagration had brought it to ruin. The population had just moved into some local caves for shelter when Sir Robert arrived. It had been decades since then. Lily wondered if they had finished rebuilding their town in new trees.

It would take a few hours to get there, so Lily set the Robyn's Nest in the correct direction facing southeast and went down to the cabin to organize the goods she had carried on board this morning.

In the mid afternoon, Lily saw a vast forest beginning to reach out endlessly in all directions. She had heard that the old village used to be near the edge of the glade where the forest started on the northwest side, so she began to make preparations to land. She began to adjust the altitude and threw her mooring anchor over the side as soon as she had clear room below. After the airship had settled, she grabbed her bag with a few provisions and her pistol, then climbed the ladder down to the ground.

She looked around at the trees waving above her. Whatever had been destroyed by the fire had been restored into new beauty. Lily tried to spot any buildings that might be in the trees, but she didn't see any right away. She moved farther under the canopy to see what she could find, making sure she could still see the Robyn's nest as she went. As she moved through the woods, she saw an area that had many trees surrounding an enormous tree in the center. This ancient tree must have been spared from the fire long ago, and the other trees grew up beside it. Walking around the huge trunk, Lily could just barely make out something far up in the top branches. It looked like a dilapidated room that was in danger of falling down to the forest floor. This must have been one of the inhabited trees. But where was the village? Lily had expected that the people would have rebuilt their tree houses by now. She saw no sign of any new buildings, or even people for that matter. Lily checked back through the trees to make sure she knew the way back to the ship, leaving a few marks for guidance, and continued further on.

Coming to an opening in the forest, Lily saw that the ground fell away into a grass covered slope. At the bottom, she observed what looked like the mouth of a cave. Along the sides of the impression, tree roots had grown out of the ground, creating makeshift, uneven stairs leading down. Lily carefully tried the first step and found that the dirt covered moss between the roots held her weight. Slowly, she made her way down the green stairway toward the opening.

At the bottom, Lily took out the lamp she had packed, filled it from a small vessel of oil, and lit it with the matches she carried. Holding this at arm's length, she proceeded to enter the cavern. The cave opening was about 10 feet wide by 8 feet high. Any light from the sun that made it down to the bottom of the indentation was weak and only gave minimal light to the inside of the cave mouth. Lily was glad of the lantern. The darkness beyond was deep and frightening, threatening to swallow any illumination that ventured in. With a bit of trepidation, Lily walked on. She began to notice that crystals on the side of the cave and in the stalactites and stalagmites would catch the light from the lantern and throw it around the room. Lily could see that the floor began to slope downwards toward the right. Following this path, she entered a long corridor that continued its downward trek. After travelling for at least a mile, the pathway opened up into a large cavern with a ceiling that Lily couldn't even see for its height. She noticed blue glimmers at the back of the cave and started moving toward them.

Suddenly, Lily noticed a moving shadow out of the corner of her eye. She spun to look, but nothing was there. Then there was more movement on the opposite side. Lily began to fear that coming into the cave was a foolish venture. She didn't know if anything living down here might want her as a meal. She began to reach for her gun when she saw two eyes looking at her from near the blue glowing crystals. The shadow was human shaped, but small. The eyes, however, were much larger than any human's eyes Lily had ever seen. Suddenly more shadows with more regular sized eyes began to appear. Lily was surrounded. She didn't want to shoot people unless she was sure they meant her harm, and she reasoned that these people could have killed her without her even knowing they were there. The group came closer and she could see human features now as men closed in on her, blinking in the lantern light. They were not much taller than Lily, and had pallid faces under dark, wavy hair. As far as she could make out, they were dressed in short tunics of what looked to be a shiny sort of leather. Gently, they began to lead her away toward the back of the cavern. Nervous, but understanding they meant her no harm by their gestures, she followed them.

One of them made motions for her to put out her lantern. She realized that the light hurt their eyes, so she extinguished it. As they walked for a while in darkness, Lily started to see that the blue glow of the crystals suffused the cave and provided a dim but very calming light that, once adjusted to it, provided enough illumination to see decently enough. A river appeared around a bend and meandered near what Lily assumed was a road. They came to a substantial group of rock buildings that children were running between while women worked nearby. Lily wondered where the child she had seen earlier had gone to. The eyes she had seen were so unusual. Watching the other youngsters playing, she noticed that some of the younger children had abnormally large eyes as well. They caught the light and shimmered blue as they glanced up at the new comer. A woman holding a baby walked by, and it also had large, piercing blue eyes. Lily stared back in astonishment as the group continued to move on.

The group finally stopped at a large house near the end of the road. They gestured for her to go inside, so Lily went through the door sized aperture and noticed that a large crystal was sitting on a table in the center of the first room, allowing her to look around in the dim light. A few flat slabs of rock sat around the table as chairs. To her left, movement made her turn her head. An elderly man with long white hair and an impressively long beard came into the room. He looked at Lily a moment and hesitatingly said "Hello?"

"You speak my language?" Lily asked, shocked.

The man answered slowly "I learned it, many years ago as a child. A man came to our village and helped us after a wildfire had destroyed our homes. He

51

stayed for a few months and taught anyone who wanted to learn. It has been a long time since I have spoken it, but I still read some of the books that the man left for me."

"That must have been Sir Robert!"

"Yes, that was his name. He left a long time ago now."

"I found his old airship and I've started travelling around to see the places from his old adventures. What happened here? Why are you living underground?"

The man smiled sadly. "I am the only one left who knows the old ways, the ways of the forest. All the new generations are afraid. They only know the stories of the fire; they have only known life in the caves. We used to call ourselves "Those Who Walk Among the Leaves". Now we are "Those Who Live Below".

Lily didn't understand this. "But trees will continue to grow, life continues on. Why will no one go up to see? It's beautiful up there."

"I know. Years ago, an expedition was made, but the forest had not yet recovered. Now, no one even tries. They have given up. They don't see the point in leaving when we have a village here. We eat fish out of the river, or lizards from the walls. We make our clothing from dried fish skins. Our eyes have adjusted to the semi darkness. I'm sure you have seen the children. They are starting to adapt to this life, very much like the fish we catch. The village sees me as venerable because I am old, but they also think I have lost my wits with age. No one would listen if I told them it was safe to live in the open air again."

Lily frowned. "Would you mind if I tried? Perhaps they would believe someone from outside the village."

"You may try if you like. Feel free to use this extra room as your own while you stay here." He said this as he pointed to a room on the right.

"Thank you. What may I call you? I'm Lily."

"I was once called 'He Who Has Seen the Sun', but no one knows what the sun is anymore. I am mostly just called Elder."

"Thank you for your hospitality, Elder" said Lily as she headed back to the door.

Outside, the group was still waiting. The elder appeared behind Lily and nodded his head in approval, so they began moving away. Lily decided to see if she could try and communicate with the few who still hung around out of curiosity. She picked up a small stone and began drawing in the dirt on the floor of the cavern. She drew trees, clouds, and the sun above them. She said "There are trees again above, and a beautiful sky.

You could have fresh air and growing things again."
They looked at her in confusion. The Elder came up
behind her and started to translate. When they
understood, they all laughed.

"They say 'you are speaking children's stories'."

"Tell them that I just came from there, so I had
to have seen it," Lily said, frustrated.

Again, the Elder translated her message. The
men looked thoughtful for a moment, but then laughed
again. One of them spoke to the Elder.

"He says 'Even if what you said is true, why
should we leave? There are only fires and destruction
up above. We have all heard the stories. Down here
we are safe'."

Lily felt her famous temper starting to rise, but
realized that yelling would do no good here. She
thanked the Elder and asked if he would speak to some
of the others with her. He nodded and they moved
back down the road.

The first person they came across was a woman
sitting on a rock, fishing by the side of the river. Beside
her was a stone bowl of pale grey fish that had large,
protruding eyes. She looked up as Lily and the Elder
came over, with a confused expression on her face. Lily
kneeled down so she was in the woman's line of sight.
As she spoke, the Elder translated. "Hello, I'm Lily. I

came from above ground. Aren't you tired of just eating these fish every day? In the forest, there are many animals, birds, fruits, and vegetables that you could catch or grow for your food. You could walk in the sun and enjoy the breeze. Would you like to go see it?"

The woman looked up at the Elder and he translated back to Lily: "Who is this woman? She knows nothing of how things work here. The river and cave provide our food and clothing. We need nothing else. Her stories of forests are from long ago. We cannot have that back even if we wanted it." The woman shooed her away as she went back to catching fish.

Lily looked at the Elder as they walked away. "She's right. I know nothing about your life down here. I have no right to tell them what they should be doing. I just know how wonderful it sounded to live in the village the way it was before, and what a joy it is to walk in the sun. They really don't care about the forest anymore, do they?"

"No, not anymore. And it was wonderful. The children here used to pretend that they were living in the trees, but soon enough not many remembered what trees were. They have made a life for themselves here, even if it is far inferior to the life we had in the forest. Many people would rather live as we do now in relative safety than face the fear of the unknown, even if it is better than what they have. "

The Elder motioned to her. "Come down here by the river. I want to show you something."

Lily followed him down to the water, where she could make out a stone boat floating in the river, reflecting the blue light of the cave walls. It had beautiful carvings that showed true craftsmanship.

"A stone boat? Won't it sink if we get in it?" Lily asked.

"Not any more than a wooden boat." The Elder laughed. "They are all prone to sinking if poorly made or handled."

This seemed reasonable, but Lily was still nervous to enter until she saw him get in and sit down without incident. Lily followed. He was an old man, but was still rather spry for his age.

Taking a stone oar, the Elder shoved off and made his way out into the middle of the river. Lily looked down into the water and saw faintly glowing blue crystals down there as well. The houses receded and they travelled into a large open cavern. Lily gasped. On the ceiling, millions of tiny blue crystals glowed like stars, reflecting in the water below.

"It's not the same as the sky" said the Elder "but it's still a glimpse of beauty here under the earth."

So there are even wonders down here. She wished the people could have both this and the real night sky, though.

Arriving back at the Elder's home, Lily sat on one of the rock slabs and thought. She had never met people so stubborn. She remembered the time her Grandmother Winnie had said the same thing about her, come to think of it. I guess it's just human nature. She tried to think of something that might change their mind, but she knew it was probably hopeless. She wasn't even sure if they could go up now, with the genetic changes that were already starting to take place. She decided to stay the night and start heading back to the Robyn's Nest the next day. She didn't want to walk through the forest in the dark.

That evening, or so Lily assumed by her watch, she and the Elder had a meal of some of the pop-eyed fish. They really didn't taste bad, even raw as they were, but they looked awful. They spoke of his youth when Sir Robert had visited and remembered some of his tales together. She asked him why the village had moved underground to begin with.

"Often, during bad storms, we would come down to these caves to stay safe from the strong winds that would shake the trees. We had lighting strikes before, but nothing as bad or as close as the one that occurred before Sir Robert came. There was almost nothing left of our homes, even after our best efforts. I was only a child, but I remember the adults forming a chain from the river, carrying bucket after bucket, but the flames were too intense. We finally fled to the caves."

"How sad, to lose everything, even your way of life."

"We made do the best we could. We learned how to catch and eat what we could find in the caves and dry fish skin to make leather. The temperature never changes, either, so we don't need warm clothes."

Lily thanked the Elder for his hospitality and headed off to bed. It wasn't the most comfortable room she had ever had, but the cave moss over the rock bed wasn't too bad. She was soon asleep.

In the morning, she and the Elder ate another strange, raw fish for breakfast. She began to gather her things, but the Elder stopped her for a moment. "Do you think you could take me with you outside? I am old, my wife passed many years ago, and we had no children. There is nothing for me here. I want to see the sun again before I die."

"I'd be happy to, but what will you do outside alone? Do you think anyone else from the village will come with you?"

"Perhaps eventually they may. Who knows? We cannot make up the minds of others, only our own.

And I spent all of last night deciding what I wanted to do with the rest of what time I have left."

Lily helped the Elder gather his few belongings and headed into the village. As they moved along, the Elder gathered people into a group to say his goodbyes. Some people laughed, and others looked concerned. Some acted like they were trying to dissuade him. Others cried and hugged him.

Afterward, Lily asked what had been said.

"I let them know that the time had come for me to live my life above ground again. I told them I would miss them, but that they were always welcome to come and visit me to see the forest. Some were scared and some were sad, but they knew they could not stop me once I had made this decision."

They walked up the road that led to the cave entrance. Thankfully it was a direct path, though winding, to make it back to the area where she had first met the villagers. When they had made it that far, Lily asked if she might light her lamp to guide them the rest of the way until they could see daylight from the entrance. The Elder conceded and kept his eyes shielded, knowing he would have to get used to the bright light again soon. Lily moved ahead to find the slope that she had taken down, and they picked their way up through the rocks to the opening. Here the

Elder had to take a few minutes to adjust his eyes to the sunshine. But, oh, the smile on his face.

"Why did it take me so long to come back?" he said.

"It's easy to get into a habit and not want to change it. It's also hard to leave everything and everyone you know behind. You've done a very brave thing to come back here."

The Elder laughed. "I don't feel brave. I feel like a foolish old man who wants to live his childhood again. I suppose there's nothing really wrong in that, though"

"No, not at all," Lily said through a grin.

They walked into the grassy opening before the cave and Lily took the Elders arm as she helped him up the mossy steps to the higher ground.

The first order of business was to find or make a shelter for the Elder. It would be too much for him to live up in the trees again, so they looked for a decent area on the ground. Lily had boards and nails back on the airship for repairs, so they went and gathered what they needed and spent the rest of the day working on a small hut. When evening came, they had a decent one room home built. As the sun set, they started a roaring fire near the entrance to cook some of the provisions Lily had grabbed off of the Robyn's Nest.

The Elder sighed happily. "I haven't done this since I was a boy. We used to gather nuts from the trees and roast them over the fire while telling each other terrible ghost stories. What fun we had."

"That sounds wonderful. My Grandmother Winnie would take me camping when I was little. Sometimes Grandfather Rex would come along as well if he had time. We would always roast marshmallows. Grandmother Winnie would tell me adventure stories of Sir Robert, and Grandfather Rex would tell scary stories that would make my hair stand on end, but I secretly enjoyed them. I miss them both so much."

They both stared into the fire for a while, alone in their own thoughts. After a time, Lily asked the Elder what it was like living in the forest village as a child.

"We were always building and expanding the village. Every time we cut down a tree, we would plant another to take its place. The treetops were our homes, but we moved all through the forest grounds as well to hunt wild animals and fish from the streams. We always tried to be careful with fire and would clean out dead brush, but when the great storm came and lighting hit the trees, there was not much we could do. We saved what we could and escaped to the caves. That's all I have known for these past decades. I will have to remember how to live up here once again."

"I'm sure it will come back to you, and I will help with whatever I can for now." Lily handed the Elder an extra blanket from her stash and wished him goodnight.

The next day, the two spent the morning wandering through the near-by area to see what edible vegetation they could find. There were a few berry bushes that were safe to eat, and a few wild root vegetables that could be cultivated. They dug a small garden and Lily shared a few turnip and bean seeds she found amongst the seed bags she had brought to trade with on her journey. There was enough sunlight in the clearing that the plants should be able to grow well.

Over the next week, Lily and the Elder made fishing nets and poles to catch the local trout. He had remembered doing this as a boy. While Lily still had her gun handy, she was loathe to use up any of her bullets unless she was in danger or unable to hunt with any other means. So far, there also didn't seem to be any wildlife nearby larger than a fox that could endanger the Elder and his new home.

One night, while sitting at the fire, Lily and the Elder heard a noise in his garden. A rabbit had found its way in and was helping itself to some of the seeds buried in the freshly turned dirt. While the Elder said he was by no means against eating small game, they had plenty of food at the moment and he would prefer to catch the animal unharmed. They shooed it off for now, and agreed to meet the next morning for the Elder so show Lily how to build a small trap.

After roasting a few fish for breakfast, the Elder took Lily to the riverside and had her gather as many young reeds as she could find. He wove them together, stopping to remember just how each piece needed to combine with the next. He hadn't done this in years, he told Lily. Using bark and some sticks, he fashioned a door and a small trigger that snapped it shut when an animal entered. Lily was impressed. They spent the rest of the day fixing the garden and planting a few more seeds. They didn't see the rabbit again, so they wondered if they had been successful in scaring it off. Lily wanted to see the trap in action, but was also glad if the rabbit wasn't going to be a problem again.

Right before dusk began to fall, the Elder took the small trap, propped the door open, and set the trigger, placing a few vegetables inside that Lily had supplied. They hid around the side of his hut, peeking out to see if the rabbit returned. Sure enough, it hopped out of the woods and made its way toward the garden. Nearing the trap, it stood on its hind legs, its pink nose twitching. It circled the trap, smelling the plants inside. Deciding that nothing was amiss, he made his way inside. As soon as he hit the trigger, the door closed abruptly behind him.

"Well done, Elder! It worked!" Lily said, patting the Elders shoulder.

63

"Just like I remembered," he said with a smile.

Lily took the trap across the river, wading in knee deep. The Elder had remembered that rabbits don't like crossing water unless forced to, so he hoped that it would be enough of a deterrent. Hopefully any more creatures would also stay away. Climbing a hill, Lily released the rabbit and made her way back.

While the Elder had to be at least in his early 80s, he got around fairly easily for a man his age, if not a bit slowly. Being in the sunlight again also brought back a vitality that he hadn't had in years. He told Lily one evening, "I am so happy to have met you. Thank you again for your help. I feel like I have a true home again. I can't say I won't miss you when you leave, but I can say I don't think I will be lonely here. I have the wind, the sun, and the trees again. I never dreamed that I could walk back here once more. I feel like my youth has been given back to me for a time."

Lily was still worried about him being on his own. "What if something happens to you? Who will take care of you? Winter is still a ways off and I am heading south, so I'm not too worried about the weather if you would like me to stay longer. I want to make sure you have everything you need. "

The Elder smiled. "You are always welcome here."

Lily stayed on for a month. She and the Elder walked the woods, fished, trapped, and foraged. The Elder taught her how to skin and dry the animals and fish they caught, and soon he had a good store of food. Lily even gave him some of her salt and an extra cooking pot. One evening, toward sunset, the pair were startled to hear a noise coming through the brush. Lily jumped up and placed her hand on her gun, peering through the darkening woods. Out walked a man, one of the members of the group that had met Lily in the cave. He looked bewildered. He saw Lily, and then noticed the Elder sitting by the fire. He burst into a grin and came to sit next to him. Lily sat down, feeling a bit dizzy in her shock. Someone had actually ventured above ground!

The newcomer and the Elder sat and spoke for a little while, the Elder explaining every so often what they were saying so Lily could understand. The man, Kai, had been worried about the Elder since he had left. He finally overcame his fear of leaving the cave, and came up to see what had happened to him. He had never expected this! When he exited the cave, the sun was still too bright, even in its last rays. The sunshine hurt his eyes and it took him a while before he could see where he was going. He had noticed a glowing light through the trees, and followed it to the hut. He was amazed at everything they had built.

Over dinner, the Elder explained everything to Kai. He was still unsure of the world outside of the cave, but he was fascinated. The next day, Kai went with the Elder to see the garden, and the stream, and everything Lily and he had built. Kai still had trouble with the sunlight, but he said how nice it felt on his skin. He said no one else wanted to come. They thought he was crazy, too. He planned on going back and telling them what he had seen. He promised to be back soon, though. Maybe some others would come with him.

In the morning, Kai went back to the cave, and Lily decided she should be going as well. "I know you have someone looking after you now, Elder, and I feel much better about leaving you here. I hope more people come up here and visit you. It may be too much for the some, though."

"I have everything I need. Go, with my blessings. Remember that you always have a home here, if your travels lead you back."

They embraced each other, Lily trying not to cry, then she walked back to the Robyn's Nest. After checking her inventory and performing her safety checks, so looked once more back toward the woods, where a small wisp of smoke was rising, and let the airship glide back up and away, toward a new destination.

CHAPTER SIX

Lily consulted her map. It wouldn't hurt to resupply the ship after using much of her food during her sojourn in Avoclaide. The nearest area that had a major city was a group of islands to the southwest of here, the Tartian archipelago. She had never been to the sea, and she had always wanted to sit on a beach. She had only seen pictures and heard about what they were like from Grandmother Winnie. From the stories about Sir Robert, she remembered he had fought air pirates around the islands, bringing down one of their ships with a cannon that he had at the time, and scaring off the rest. With good weather, it would only take her a few days to get there. She had plenty of fuel and provisions, so she wouldn't need to stop. She looked over the horizon and didn't see anything alarming, so she set the wheel and went below deck for a while to read one of the adventure novels Hannah had snuck aboard, and dream of the ocean.

Over the next few days, the land below the ship began to show less and less trees and large rivers started to be seen. The air grew warmer and more humid. Lily dropped her altitude a bit and checked her compass to make small adjustments. On the third day after setting out, the ocean, in all its blue green glory, came into view. Lily was spellbound. She knew it was big, but she had no idea it would be this big! Maps did it no justice. Toward the afternoon, she glimpsed what she thought was the first island in the chain. She was aiming for the last island, where the largest city was. She knew there used to be an shipyard here as well during Sir Robert's days, but not as many used them anymore, since the upkeep on the new models was usually too much for most people. Everybody else mostly took commercial airships, boats, and trains, so the private airfields for personal airships were sometimes hard to come by, or so Collin had told Lily.

As she neared the final island, and the city of Fanea, she could make out tall, brightly painted buildings, beautiful beaches, and a trail leading off to a jungle. Looking for a place to land, Lily noticed a large area on the outskirts of the city that could at least hold her ship. Seeing the familiar airfield flags as she descended, she knew this was the old shipyard Sir Robert must have used. She was glad it was still here. Even though her ship was patterned off of a boat, she didn't want to find out how seaworthy it was...or wasn't. Men on the ground directed her to a spot and helped her tie down the ship. Glancing around, she noticed she was the only one docked there. She paid a small fee out of the money the Applegates had given her to the man at the gate and left to explore.

She had seen there was a large beach off to the south, so she headed there first. Coming to the edge of the sand, she took her boots and stockings off and let her toes sink in. It was hot, but there was a delicious coolness underneath the surface. Lily made her way down to the lapping waves and rinsed her feet off, wading in to her calves. The salt water stung a bit, but it was so refreshing. It amazed her that only a few days ago, she was in a deep forest, and now she was relaxing on a beach. The world was an astounding place.

Down the shore a bit, a group of boys were playing with a ball near the lapping waves. They were around the ages of twelve to fourteen, and were determined to ignore a younger girl, probably one of their sisters. Lily decided to wander down the water's edge, and as she passed the group, one of them missed the ball and it landed in the surf. With quick reflexes, Lily was able to grab it before the ocean took it out too far. As she tossed it back to them, one of the younger boys asked if she wanted to play, too. Having nothing else to do on this lovely day, she joined in throwing the ball around, making sure to include the little girl, who was probably around 6. They were good natured kids, and after laughing with them for a bit, she continued her ramble.

Coming back up onto the cobblestone road, she brushed off her feet and put her stockings and boots back on. There was a charming shopping area here. She had never really had much time or money to shop for the fun of it. Finding a small bakery, she went in and purchased what she was told was a guava pastry. She took a bite of the flaky crust and savored the sweet fruit filling. Heavenly! She had never had anything like it before. Purchasing a meat bun for dinner, she finished up her window shopping and went back to the beach to find a good spot to watch the sunset.

Past the town, she found a promenade that included a boardwalk out over the water. Lily found an unoccupied wooden bench and sat down to enjoy her bun and watch as the sun slowly sank into the sea. She had never been this relaxed. The sky turned pink at first, and then flared out into a brilliant orange as the light faded. Thoroughly pleased, Lily walked back to the Robyn's Nest to sleep in her own bed. Before turning in, she made sure to write a note to the Applegates and tell them about her journey so far. She knew they would be worrying.

When Lily woke up, the first thought she had was to go back to the bakery and get another guava pastry. She didn't want to wantonly spend what money she had, but this was too good to miss. After she washed and dressed, she paid the airfield manager for another day and headed back to town. She arranged for some supplies to be dropped off at the shipyard, and then headed toward the bakery. After Lily purchased the coveted pastry, she found a small post office to mail her letter, and then went back to the boardwalk to enjoy the morning sea breeze. As Lily walked over the worn planks, she noticed the group of boys again, with the little girl trailing behind. They were carrying fishing poles, intending to try their luck off the side of the pier.

Passing by, Lily heard the tallest boy say to the little girl "Mary, stop following us. You don't even like to fish."

"Do so!" cried Mary. "Mama said you have to be nice to me, Tommy! I'll tell if you don't let me come."

Tommy rolled his eyes and continued on with his friends, obviously deciding it wasn't worth an argument. Lily smiled to herself and continued her walk.

That evening, Lily decided to walk the town again and see what other local foods she could find. Turning a corner, the aromatic scents of garlic and spices wafted towards her. There was a small café, brightly lit with hanging lamps. Lily got a table for herself and asked for the specialty, which was a baked local fish. They even got her to try an oyster on the house after she told the waiter that she had never had one before. The site of it made her nervous, but on assurances from the wait staff, she squeezed some lemon on it and threw back her head as she swallowed. It had a wonderful minerality to it that the lemon juice complemented perfectly. She ordered another, and decided these were quite fun for a treat now and then. Her baked fish came out smelling of saffron and herbs, and flaked at the slightest touch of her fork. Delicious!

After dinner, she followed a group out on to the beach who had gathered to watch the stars. She sat down on the cooling sand and watched a falling star streak through the black sky. Constellations came into view, and white stars glittered in the vast distance. Lily remembered the times when she camped with her grandparents, and how Grandpa Rex would tell her the names of the different constellations. She had good memories to follow her back to the ship that night.

After loading her supplies onto the ship the next morning, Lily, out of habit now, went back to her favorite bakery. As she was paying, she saw the group of children heading to the beach with buckets. Again, Mary tagged along, swinging her little blue bucket as her small legs tried to keep up with the long stride of the boys.

"Tommy, wait! You're going too fast!" she panted.

"Why don't you go play with your own friends? Go have a tea party or something."

"No, that's ALL they ever want to do, and I'm tired of it. Please let me build sand castles with you!"

Tommy shrugged and kept walking. Mary followed with a huge grin on her face.

Lily laughed at the pair, and made her way out of town toward the walking path she had seen when she landed a few days ago. It was a trail through the small jungle on the far side of the island. The worn dirt path led through trees covered with vines, where small, brightly colored birds sang in the branches. A distant noise, much like a train, caught her ears and grew louder as she travelled on. After walking around a few large boulders, Lily came across a small pond that was fed by a tall waterfall crashing down from a cliff. A rainbow appeared in the mist and spray that came up as the rushing water hit the still pool beneath. Lily stood there a moment to enjoy the site before continuing on her way. The path ended behind the village near a small beach dotted with small stones and shells, so Lily picked up a few souvenirs before returning. She began thinking of fresh seafood again and headed back to the restaurant from last night to enjoy more delicacies.

The following morning was a bright, clear day and Lily could see one of the nearby islands in the distance. She could make out the green of the trees and also saw a dark mass rising up from the forest. At intervals, it looked like dark red-orange fire was appearing at the top. Was this a volcano? She had read about them, but had never seen one up close. Was this the beginning of an eruption? She wasn't too worried, since it was on another island, but she wondered what exactly to expect if it began erupting in full.

Lily took another stroll down the shore, making her way closer to the volcano island to see if she could get a better view. A crowd had gathered toward that end of the beach, as others had seen the telltale signs of the eruption. She overheard a few of the men saying they had expected as much. No one seemed surprised or concerned, so Lily decided to just enjoy the show. As she moved through the crowd to find the best vantage point, she saw Mary standing with a woman. She was crying so hard that her mother, who was trying to listen to her, could barely make out what she was saying. Curious, Lily got close enough so that she could hear.

"They're gone!" screamed small Mary.

"Who are, dear?" the patient woman asked.

"Tommy and his friends. He told me not to say anything, but I just know they will be killed!" At this she burst into fresh tears.

Now Lily was alarmed. Some of the nearby groups had also heard her, and began to ask where they had gone. It was eventually learned that Tommy and his friends had snuck off early that morning, knowing there was going to be an eruption. Wanting to get a good look, they took one of their rafts and sailed off to watch from the lagoon near the volcano. Soon a mad rush began, and Tommy's father and the other boys' parents ran off to get boats to go bring them back. At that moment, the volcano exploded, sending lava high into the air and bubbling down the side of the mountain, into the lagoon. Fearing that the boats wouldn't be able to get through the flow of lava, Lily raced back to her ship and got it into the air in record time.

Sailing up over the town, she soon saw the volcano below her, the lava cascading down and sizzling and steaming as it hit the water. The sulfur fumes made her cough. She brought the Robyn's Nest lower, and saw that the lava was blocking the entrance to the lagoon, trapping the boys in and their parents out. Desperately looking around, she finally saw small shapes waving their arms. They were all gathered on a nearby rock that protruded out into the water.

A fresh burst of boulders and compressed molten rock shot out of the volcano's mouth and made the Robyn's Nest its next target. Lily was able to swerve to the left to avoid a collision, a large stone narrowly missing the bow. She had to figure out how to get to the boys in the safest manner. If she went down too, no one would be able to get to them in time.

Skirting the volcano on the left, she looked to see if there was a large space for her to land close enough to the boys to get them out of harm's way. She circled the area for a moment, only seeing jagged rocks and pits. Worry knit her brow as she looked at the boys, still frantically calling for help. She was going to have to try something desperate.

Not knowing if she would be able to keep the ship steady enough, Lily took the airship down as low as she could and threw the rope ladder over the side. She yelled down to ask if they could climb up. They nodded their assent and clambered up the side as she tried to keep the ship as still as possible.

Tommy was the last one to start to climb up, wanting to make sure his friends were ahead of him first. The boy ahead of him lost his grip, starting to fall back down to the rocks. Tommy reached out his hand and grabbed his wrist, helping him to clamber back onto the ladder, making sure he safely made it to the top. Tommy then pulled himself over the side of the ship and landed on his back, exhausted.

"Are you all safe?" she asked as Tommy lay gasping on deck.

He nodded. "Yes, we're all here. Our raft didn't make it though. It got caught in the lava and started to burn so we had to jump overboard and make our way to that rock. I think maybe we got too close."

"Yes, I think maybe you did. I'm glad you're not hurt." This was all Lily could trust herself to say on the subject. She would leave anything else to their parents.

She brought the ship back around and headed toward the airfield. By this time, the whole town had gathered there after witnessing the events. Lily landed and helped the boys down to the ground to find their families. Mary found Lily and gave her a big hug, while her mother and the other parents thanked her profusely for her help. Embarrassed, she just smiled and said she was happy she could help.

As the crowd left, Lily watched the parents scolding then hugging their children. She smiled. It reminded her of the time when, the same age as Mary, Grandmother Winnie had found her hanging from her skirt, trapped on a tree limb that she had been climbing. She had told her again and again not to climb that tree, because it was too tall and she could get hurt. Lily, flushed with indignation from the most recent admonition, decided that Grandmother Winnie could not possibly know better than herself, so climb the tree she did. Thus she found herself, upside down and bleeding from a gash in her leg. Grandmother Winnie removed her from the branch, hugged her, and said, very quietly but firmly "I don't tell you not to do things because I want to make you unhappy. I say them so you do not get hurt. Nothing would injure me more than for something to happen to you." Lily had sobbed and sobbed, not because of the cut she had suffered from her fall, but because she had disappointed her Grandmother.

Back in town, Lily kept meeting people who wanted to shake her hand and thank her. While this was kind, she also realized that her relaxing time here was over. Lily was also concerned about the smoke blackening the sky. The winds were mostly blowing it away from Fanea, but if the winds shifted, it could cause problems for navigation. She picked up a few more pastries and watched another beautiful sunset, determined to leave the next morning.

That evening, back in her room, Lily plotted her next course. If she continued in a southeastern direction, she could make her way to Allegande and see what wonders she could trade for. It was a huge, ancient city with a bazaar that went on for miles, or so Collin had said during his tale of Sir Robert. She might even be able to meet the Yurisvenians. Lily thought it would be fun to find out.

CHAPTER SEVEN

Waking to a pink and purple sunrise, Lily stretched and greeted the day. After going through all her checks and setting her course, she sailed off once again. The sky was blue and clear with only light winds, so she made her way easily to Allegande over the next day and a half, landing in their airfield as the sun went down.

The bazaar was closed for the evening, so Lily stayed on the Robyn's Nest and prepared the items she was planning on trading the next day. She still had all of the sugar left, but she had given half of the seeds to the Elder in Avoclaide for his garden. No matter. She still had plenty and could hardly wait to see what she could bargain for.

After breakfast, Lily left the airfield, borrowing a cart and paying the fee for her stay as she left. Finding the main road, she followed the stream of people into the bazaar. Collin was right! It stretched endlessly out before her, twisting here and there and overflowing into side streets. She saw gold platters, delicate, ornate jars, heaps of aromatic spices, rugs...the list was endless. Almost anything she could have thought of was here for sale, to be haggled or bargained for. Lily had never had to barter for anything in her life. She paid what things cost. She hoped she wouldn't get taken in for a fool here, but she very much feared that was her fate.

Pushing through the crowd for two hours and perusing the goods, Lily finally pinned her hopes on a beautifully woven green and purple blanket. She approached the woman running the stall and offered her one bag of sugar for it. The woman waved her hands at her, and said two bags at least. Pondering this, and having no way of knowing what was fair, Lily was about to hand them over. All of a sudden, her attention was drawn to a tall man in elegant robes who appeared beside her and put his hand out to stop her transaction.

Surprised, she put the bags down and looked at him wonderingly. He smiled and bowed slightly. She nodded in return, not quite sure what to think. He gesticulated to the woman, and she aggressively motioned back, insisting on two bags still. He continued on in this way, making gestures to the merchant, until the woman finally took one bag from Lily and handed her the blanket, 2 silk shirts, and a small, round rug. She was astonished. Turning to the man to thank him, he bowed again and walked away.

Lily felt sure that the man was from Yurisvenia. His quiet gestures made it almost assured. She looked to see if she could find where he had gone, but the crowd had enveloped him. It was a pity that she knew none of their signs, but she was content to know that he had heard and acknowledged her thanks.

After buying a few bread loaves that were thankfully cash only, Lily took her purchases back to the ship. She laid the new blanket on her bed and it immediately brightened the space. The new rug worked perfectly on the bedroom floor as well. Unable to resist, she tried the new shirts on to see how they fit. They were perfect, and felt soft and light on her skin. What a blessing the Yurisvenian man had seen her and offered to help! She would have never known one bag of sugar could buy all this.

In the morning, Lily ate some of her bread with honey from her stores and delighted in the fluffy sweetness. Back to the bazaar she went, intending only to look this time and not bring all her offerings with her. She could decide later to trade if something caught her eye. She rambled from stall to stall, seeing things that had gone unnoticed yesterday. She paused at some earrings that had piqued her interest, and as she looked up, she saw again the man that had helped her the other day. She walked up to him and the group he was with, and he bowed in acknowledgment of her. She pulled out her writing pad, brought on purpose in case she ran into him again. She turned to the first page, handing it to him as she thanked him again for his help, and asked if he was from Yurisvenia. He nodded his affirmation. He wrote to ask if she would like him to show her around. She nodded eagerly. He introduced his companions, who turned out to be his wife and brother-in-law. Lily introduced herself, and found out the man's name was Adam, his wife Sofia, and her brother Jamal.

They continued through the stalls, Adam or Sofia every now and again showing her items of interest. In the afternoon, they took her to a coffee house where she had a brew that was dark and spicy, along with a sweet, orange roll. What luxury! They even insisted on paying, even over her protests. These people were so incredibly kind to her, who was really just a stranger to them. She had told them a bit about her travels and why she was on her journey. They had also heard stories about Sir Robert as he was still respected in Yurisvenia. That evening, as they were about to part, Sofia took Lily's notebook and asked if she would like to come back to the village with them the next day. She graciously accepted, and they said their goodnights.

Back on the Robyn's Nest, Lily could hardly believe the opportunity presented to her. She realized that she really should be writing a diary about her travels, abashed that she hadn't thought of this before. She sat down that night and wrote down everything that had happened to her since buying the Robyn's Nest. She wrote of everyone she had met and the places she had seen. It really hadn't been long since she had left the Applegate's, only a little over a month, but it had felt like years to a girl who had hardly been anywhere in her life before this. She closed her diary for the evening and packed it in the bag she had started for her trip the next day, looking forward to adding more adventures.

Gathering her things and heading toward the meeting point, Lily wondered how a whole community of people couldn't, or didn't, speak. She had known of deaf people that were also mute, but she had never seen hearing people that didn't use speech. It fascinated her. She didn't want to ask rude questions, so she just planned to go and learn about their culture and appreciate them for who they are.

After making a deal at the shipyard for her extended stay and taking a few supplies from her stores, Lily headed off to meet Adam and his family. She greeted them with a wave as she approached the meeting point, and they began their journey. They took a path that started on the outskirts of the city and meandered up into the mountains. The day was hot, but not oppressive. Lily was still glad she had grabbed a hat. There was no reason to court sunstroke.

The trail was wide and beaten smooth from years of travel. Lily noticed a gradual ascent beginning after about a mile. After 2 hours, they could look down over the bazaar and watch people milling about far below. Lily wasn't especially afraid of heights, but she also preferred not to get too close to the edge. It was one thing to be on the deck of an airship that had railings, and a completely different feeling of being on the edge of a steep hill with nothing to prevent her from tumbling down.

The evening quietly descended, and the four travelers stopped in a clearing for the night. Adam and Jamal cut branches and started a fire while Lily helped Sofia lay out blankets and prepare a light meal. As they sat around the fire, Adam began signing a story that Sofia kindly translated in Lily's notebook. He told of an ancient nomad who united warring tribes to protect their land from an invading tyrant. The nomad became king, and peace followed his reign. As Adam spoke, he acted out each character in mime, the shadows from the fire playing across his face.

Afterwards, Jamal unpacked a type of flute that he was carrying and played one of the sweetest, saddest tunes Lily had ever heard. Lily stared into the heart of the flames, listening to the notes as they floated up with the smoke. They all slept that night around the fire, wrapped tight in their blankets, lulled by the crackling of the burning branches.

The smell of smoky ashes and the feel of sun on her skin woke Lily the next morning. She rolled out of her blanket and washed her face in a bowl that Sofia provided for her. The group stoked the fire back up for a small breakfast, Lily sharing the bread she had brought. The group then re-packed their belongings and renewed their walk.

The ground began to become more level while short, bushy trees appeared. A brook came into view on their left and gurgled its way down the hillside. Above their heads, a bird with a fantastically feathered head flew by. Seeing Lily's interest, Sofia tried to sign what it was, then wrote in Lily's book that she didn't know the written name for it, but her village saw them often.

In the afternoon, they stopped by a well along the side of the road to replenish their water supplies and finish off the rest of the food they had brought. They would arrive at the village soon enough. Lily wondered if she was making herself a burden, coming along with them like this to a place where she had no home. She was sure they would not have asked, though, if they had not wanted her to come. If Sir Robert had done so, then Lily figured she might as well do the same. She would do her best to be helpful when possible and out of the way otherwise.

The sky grew dark, and what had started off as faint strains of music coming to them from afar soon turned into a melodious song. Lily could hear strings, percussion, winds instruments, almost a whole orchestra. None of it sounded quite like anything she had ever heard before.

The village finally came into view, and Lily saw that, if not all, at least most of the inhabitants must have been out in the square. There were couples dancing in the middle, with many people around them playing things Lily had never seen before. Some had stringed instruments beautifully carved out of wood. Others players had carved flutes or horns. The drums ranged from small, handheld contraptions to enormous ones on the ground. Sitting along the sides of the square were older couples, taping their toes to the music.

Had they known they were coming? Was this a welcome? She asked Jamal, who was closest to her at that moment, and he smiled and wrote: "This is how the village is every evening. Anyone who wants to play or dance comes out to the square when the weather is nice. If it rains, you often hear music coming from each home." Every day seemed to be a celebration here!

Lily remembered Grandmother Winnie and her phonograph, which had been a wedding present from Grandfather Rex. She had been a lover of music and would play a record almost every evening. Lily thought of the times she would watch as her grandmother lovingly placed a record on the base and wound the mechanism. They would sit back and listen to a piano concerto or a dance tune, sometimes a beautiful soprano, or a thunderous baritone. Grandmother Winnie enjoyed it all. Sometimes she would twirl Lily around the room if the mood struck, or they would sit and listen attentively to a particularly soulful piece. Grandfather Rex often gifted her new records, so there was always a fresh addition to the rotation.

Grandmother Winnie had sold the phonograph after Grandfather Rex had died because it made her miss him so much that she could no longer enjoy it. Lily had suddenly been torn from the present moment and was trapped in her memories, absorbed by an emotion she hadn't intended to feel.

Sofia saw the change on Lily's face, took her hand, and squeezed it. She then ran with her out to the square and the two twirled and laughed as the music played, breaking Lily out of her momentary funk. Jamal joined the band with his flute and Adam clapped along and beamed at his wife.

After the dance, the group brought Lily to the house that they shared. It was one story and built of white blocks and plaster inlaid with exquisite carvings. She was shown to a spare room and left to arrange her things. Sofia came in to say goodnight, and wrote to ask her why she had been upset earlier. Lily said she missed her grandmother. Sofia gave her a hug, and wrote she was sorry and she understood. She gave Lily a hug and signed good night. Lily was left alone with her thoughts until morning.

At breakfast, Lily met Adam and Sofia's two children and Adam's mother, Sarah. She was a wizened old woman with silver hair and laugh-worn wrinkles around her eyes. The children, Miriam and Zechariah, were about 10 and 8 respectively. They were playful, but still well behaved. Lily watched as they all rapidly signed to each other and smiled and clapped instead of laughing.

While at the table, Lily asked if they would be willing to teach her their sign language. She offered her last bag of seed and a bag of sugar in return for lessons and accommodations while she stayed there. They refused the sugar and tried to refuse the seeds, but Lily insisted. They only took them on the agreement that they would be shared with the village, as they offered their hospitality and help freely to any visitors.

Lessons began immediately after breakfast. Sarah entertained Miriam and Zechariah while Sofia taught Lily some basic signs. Taking notes and quick sketches in her book, Lily planned to study them later as well. She learned "hello", "how are you", "I am fine", and "goodbye", to start out with. Sofia taught her a few nouns as well, pointing to different objects and making signs to correspond. Some were more difficult than others, but Lily caught on fairly quickly.

For their afternoon meal, Lily asked if she might help so she could learn how they cooked. Sarah was happy to have her in the kitchen and showed her how to make a roasted lamb shank with vegetables. It was tender and flavorful, with a delightful spice to it. Lily wrote this down, too. She might as well collect recipes on her travels. She already had her favorite recipes from Grandmother Winnie stashed away on beautifully handwritten notes, and would love to add to them.

That evening, everyone gathered in the square as before and the music began. Adam handed Lily a small drum and helped her find the beat. She had never had the opportunity to play any instruments before, so she was nervous to join in. Adam had another drum that he played along-side her until she forgot her trepidation and began just to enjoy the rhythm. Miriam and Zachariah whirled to the melody while Sofia danced and Sarah swayed gracefully.

Day followed day in this manner, Lily learning more and more sign language and enjoying the nightly band. She saw how hard working they all were, and how they knew the importance of relaxing after a long day. As Adam had told her, when the weather was bad, the families just made their own music at home, using whatever they had. Sofia was a talented dancer, but she was also a wonderful flute player. Lily enjoyed listening to her and watching the love in Adam's eyes as he gazed at his wife while she piped out beautiful songs. Lily found joy in these evenings, but sometimes it made her miss her grandparents even more.

After Lily had been in Yurisvenia for about six weeks, Adam's family told her they were planning another market trip to gather a few things that Sarah had asked for. Knowing that she couldn't stay here forever, Lily told them she wanted to come along, and that she would take the opportunity to continue her journey. They were sad that she was leaving, but understood. Adam and Sofia tried to urge her to take supplies, but she politely refused. The one thing she couldn't bring herself to say no to was the little drum Adam had taught her to play. She gladly accepted his offer.

On the journey back to Allegande, Lily could now join in the fireside talks and concerts. Her signing was still limited, but she knew enough that she could hold basic conversations now and could understand a good portion of what was said. She had loved her time with this family that at first had seemed so quiet, but were really bursting with expression.

There was one more thing Lily wanted to do before she left. She hunted through the bazaar until she found a beautiful old phonograph and a few records. Adam helped her bargain for it with the bag of sugar she still had tried to give to them. They even threw in a few extra needles and a spare horn.

They all followed Lily to the airfield and helped her load everything aboard. After many signed goodbyes, and a hug from Sofia, Lily paid what was left for her extra time at the yard, and waved to everyone below as she took off. She was still determined to try and find Zantislan. She looked at the mark Collin had made on her map and tried her best to set her course in that direction. Everything was set and ready to go. If only she had remembered Collin's warning.

CHAPTER EIGHT

The journey went well for the first few days. The early November morning of the sixth day started off with a fantastic red sunrise. By early afternoon the rain had started. Then the winds howled around the ship. Lily anxiously began to remember what Collin had said about the fall storms. She had completely lost track of time with her new friends in Yurisvenia. If she had decided to stay longer, she would have missed most of this, but she was too impatient to keep moving. She had gotten herself into trouble once again.

Lily looked for a safe place to land, but below her in the growing dark were nothing but tightly- woven trees. A flash of lighting nearby and a deafening roar of thunder awakened her to the full peril she was in. She began lowering her altitude but she was still the highest object around. The next bolt of lightning hit the front furnace and its balloon began to deflate rapidly. She was going to land whether there was room or not.

Doing her best to keep the Robyn's Nest in one piece, Lily directed her plummet as much as possible to a small clearing she spotted below. It was still not quite wide enough and the airship scraped the trees on the way down, ending its fall by slamming into a boulder. Shaken from the landing and soaking wet, she went to seek shelter below.

The deluge ended, but now night had settled. She grabbed a lantern, lit it and walked over to where she thought the ship had hit the rock. Splintered wood greeted her in the gloom. Her heart sunk as she surveyed the damage. Thankfully, nothing serious had been destroyed, so the structure was still sound as far as she could tell. The real issue would be the furnace that was hit during the storm. Lily knew that she could get one balloon to inflate if it was still in one piece, but it would only be limping along at low altitudes, which was dangerous in these trees. She wasn't even sure if she could get back out of the small clearing she had crashed into.

Looking around the interior, she saw that her phonograph had been thrown to the ground and canned goods were scattered across the floor, rolling out of the cupboard. Lily sat in the chair at the desk that was still thankfully in one piece. She was trying to be logical and reasonable in her assessments, but she was alone, and rather frightened. It suddenly dawned on her how very alone she was. Everything she had felt since Grandmother Winnie had died came rushing back over her. She couldn't stop the tears anymore. Large, hot drops fell down her cheeks in streams, and she started sobbing and choking between wails. This wasn't about the Robyn's Nest anymore. That was just the last straw that finally broke the wall Lily had been building around her heart. She knew why she had ultimately wanted to leave Adam and his family. Every day she was there, they reminded her of everything she had lost. They were wonderful people, but the pain in her heart couldn't handle the peaceful family scenes. Lily realized even at the Applegate's she had had a hard time because they had become like grandparents to her, but she had been too distracted rebuilding the Robyn's Nest to dwell on it. Now she had nothing but her own dark thoughts and a broken ship.

She woke up the next morning, realizing that she had cried herself to sleep with her head resting on her arms. Her throat and eyes hurt and her back was sore. The only good thing she could see was that the sun was shining and the sky was clear. She got up, washed her face, and tried to reassess her situation. Climbing up on the deck, she first went to look at the furnace. It was scorched and had a hole blown in the side. Collin had shown her how to make small repairs to the ignition furnaces while he was helping her rebuild and had given her basic welding equipment for just such an emergency. She had only done small welds under his teaching though, so she didn't know if she could fix this or not. She figured at this point, her only option was to try.

She next checked the hull damage from the outside. It was smashed in, as she had seen the night before, but it was still flyable in that condition. Back inside, she picked up and re-shelved the cans and noticed she had about 3 weeks left of food and a few fresh vegetables that Sarah had given her. Her stove still worked, and her water levels were still good from her last stop. She wouldn't have to worry for a while on those accounts. She just wished she knew where she was.

Grabbing her small welding iron and some scrap metal, Lily began to go back on deck, but saw her phonograph was still lying on its side. She sat it back on a small table and replaced the needle, which had been bent in the fall. If she was going to work, she may as well listen to something to keep her mood up. She grabbed the first record she came across, something with fiery violins and drums. This should keep her distracted from her problems for a while.

Back on deck, Lily got to work trying to patch the gaping wound in her furnace. She tried to remember everything Colin had taught her, but the first few tries didn't meld properly. She sighed, listening to the strings and drums coming from below. Then something else caught her ears and eyes. She thought she saw something rustling in the tree not far from the crash. She stood up and peered into the green depths, but saw nothing else. It may have been just a squirrel, but it sounded larger. With a sense of foreboding, Lily made sure her gun was loaded and ready.

She continued working into the afternoon, pausing to change records and grab a bite here and there. The patchwork was going better, and she had seen and heard nothing else but birds around her the rest of the day. That didn't mean she felt safe. Every few moments, she would look around her to make sure nothing was coming through the trees. As evening fell, she decided it wasn't worth the risk to continue in the dark. Not that the hull was safe either. She could shut the door to the deck, but there was still the large crack in the front of the ship. The only other door that closed was to her suite, but even that didn't lock. Her best bet would to be to grab some of the boards and barricade herself in later. First, she wanted to grab something to eat.

Lily headed to the little kitchenette, placed her gun on the tiny island, and started a pot of soup boiling. She turned to grab a bowl, when her heart leapt in her chest. She had heard something jump into the hull, the boards creaking under its weight. She turned around in time to see a large, tan cat enter the kitchen. Its head was taller than the counters. She flicked her eyes over to her gun, but worried a movement might make it attack. It made a low growl and began to slink around the side of the island. Lily reached behind her for the pot, not caring that she was burning her hand as she threw the scalding liquid at the animal. It hissed and leapt backwards, pawing at its face. In the next moment she grabbed her gun and fired, but it was a wild shot and missed. The cat ran out of the kitchen with Lily chasing after it. It jumped up on the desk, sending papers flying, and turned to spring at her, claws extended. Bringing the gun up in both hands, Lily aimed

95

for center mass and hit the beast in the chest as it came down on her. It flailed for a moment on top of her and then lay still. Lily had had the wind knocked out of her when it hit her, and it took her a moment to be able to breathe again, especially with the weight of it on her chest. She rolled it to the side and stared in shock as her hands shook. Blood pooled from the wound. Lily checked herself to make sure she hadn't taken any serious damage. She was covered in blood, but most of it was the cat's. She had a few scratches on her arms and face and a burn on her hand, but nothing life threatening. She was afraid that throwing the body out of the hull would attract more predators, so she left it where it was for the moment. Food was the last thing on her mind now, so she took her gun, grabbed a few boards, and barred her door from the inside as best she could. She washed off her wounds, wrapped a few of the larger ones, and sat on her bed, facing the door for the rest of the night.

There was no window in her room, but Lily began to see what looked like faint sunlight under the door. She cautiously opened it to find the large cat's body still on the floor, the blood congealed around it. It looked like a few small animals had come in during the night and nibbled at the corpse, but no signs of a larger animal. Even so, Lily had no intention of staying here longer than she needed to. Grabbing a shovel, she carefully moved the body out of the breach that it had entered. The blood took much longer to clean up, with a stain still remaining after her troubles.

After these jobs were done, Lily grabbed what little boards she had left after helping the elder with his hut, and patched up the hole so that nothing large could get inside, or so she hoped. Returning to the furnace, Lily first looked up at the trees and around the deck, making sure nothing else was waiting for her. Her gun remained in the holster by her side, ready if anything else should leap at her. Lily patched the rest of the rent in the furnace as best she could for the next few hours. She did not plan on staying here another night if she could help it.

When she was finally happy with the patch, she tried to light the ignition again. At first, nothing happened. She tried again and it sputtered to life, but only at half power. Lily hoped this would be enough to get her airborne. The other furnace came alive with no issue, and the balloons slowly started to fill. As it expanded, it began to hit branches from the surrounding trees, sending them raining down on the deck. Lily covered her head and hoped none of them would puncture the balloons. With one furnace at only half capacity, the foremost balloon could not get to its full size, but the Robyn's Nest still began to lift off of the ground. Horrible noises came from the front as the ship ripped itself from off of the rock it had smashed into. The aft of the ship rose first, with the full balloon managing to make its way through the tree limbs. In its smaller size and with less tension, the remaining balloon began to clear the treetops without injury. Lily looked down to see the slowly receding shape of the great cat on the forest floor below. She was sorry for it, but not as glad as she was that it hadn't killed her first.

The Robyn's Nest struggled upwards to just a little above the trees, but that was enough for Lily to be able to continue her journey. She checked her maps and the stars, but couldn't quite place where she was. The only guide she had left was her compass, so she set it due south again and limped on, praying no more storms would hit her on the way.

CHAPTER NINE

After an hour, the forest gave way to empty fields, then a long beach, followed by open water reaching out on every side. Lily knew that with the large hole in the ship, she would not be able to make a water landing. If anything else happened to the Robyn's Nest, she may not make it back to shore.

Being so low in the sky, Lily could look down into the ocean and watch creatures swim by. A large school of silver fish swam close to the surface, and then a pod of dolphins leapt around them, herding them into a tight ball and then taking turns feeding on them. A group of whales approached right before twilight, spraying water up so high it almost reached the ship.

As night came down, Lily began to worry that she would miss sight of land. She was incredibly tired after her ordeal last night and her work all day, but she didn't think she could take a break yet. She lit her lanterns and kept looking over the side into the darkness, straining her eyes for any sight of trees or sand. Even in her anxious state, Lily's limbs began to drag, and her head began snapping up as she desperately tried to stay awake. The morning sun found her sleeping slumped against the mast, unable to win her battle.

Lily was startled awake as sea birds screamed over her head. She realized that they wouldn't be out too far from land, so she may be getting close to something. Unwilling to stop her vigil for breakfast, Lily looked about her, worried she may have passed land in the night. She couldn't tell if the birds were coming or going from somewhere, but they seemed to have been traveling away from the area she was now heading. After a few hours, a dark spot appeared on the horizon, off to the left. Lily ran to grab her binoculars and peered through them. She couldn't make much out from this distance, but she was definitely getting close to something. The shape gradually got bigger and the binoculars began to make out trees. Land! Looking at her map, Lily tried to determine where she might be. Collin's mark would be around this area if she was in the right part of the ocean, but she also could have been thrown off course too far left or right during the storm.

The region began to look like an island, or possibly a peninsula. Drifting closer, Lily looked down and could see what looked like mountains under the water. Zantislan was supposed to be surrounded by the same kind of formation. She began to hope she had finally reached her destination. Nearing the beach, Lily could see the water just quietly lapped the shore, with no crashing waves. She prepared to land on the beach, threw her anchor down, and looked up to see a group of people coming towards her. They walked at a leisurely gait, and carried no weapons. Fearing she may scare them, and also hoping she wasn't making a foolish mistake, Lily undid her harness and left her gun onboard as she climbed down the ladder.

Lily waved to show she was friendly and unarmed, and the group waved back as they came closer. Finally they stopped in front of her, and a man and woman stepped forward. The man greeted her by saying "Hello, and welcome to Zantislan."

CHAPTER TEN

Lily gaped for a moment, and then remembered herself. "Thank you!" she replied. "I have been looking for you for a long time." She had finally reached her goal, and almost in the same manner that Sir Robert had himself!

She followed the group to their nearby village through the palm trees. She was barely aware of herself as she looked around at the lush vegetation, singing birds, and white beach. This was everything she had wanted since she was a little girl. Overwhelmed, she began to feel tears streaming down her face, but she didn't mind anymore if anyone saw her cry. The group led her to an open area of the town where many people were gathered. The woman who had approached her on the beach asked her name, and then told the villagers "This is Lily."

The man said something Lily didn't understand, and everyone sat down. While in her stupor earlier, Lily hadn't noticed that many of the people here were bilingual. Sir Robert must have taught them as he had taught the people in Avoclaide. Lily was offered a seat on a blanket near the front of the group.

The man asked her how she knew Sir Robert. She realized the Robyn's Nest must be very familiar to them, even after this much time. Lily explained how she knew of him, and how she had acquired his ship. She spoke of her Grandmother Winnie, and of her desire to explore like Sir Robert had. She told them of her journey, of the people she had met, and of the dangers she had faced. She said the main purpose of her travels had been to get here. The man, who Lily found was named Malosi, would occasionally stop her and speak in his native language to the crowd. He explained to her that some of the people only spoke their native language and some ideas and words did not express the meaning as well in her language. Lily found this fascinating. She had never thought about words being better expressed in another language.

His sister, Kiana, told Lily, "Everyone here knows and loves the stories of Sir Robert. He lived with us until his death at 102. Would you like to visit his grave?" This shocked Lily. She knew he couldn't possibly still be alive, she had just never thought about visiting his grave. "I would be honored," she said.

Kiana led her through the trees to a small glade, where there was a cemetery filled with beautifully carved stones. On one large boulder near the center was written "Here lies Sir Robert Pettigrew. He lived the best he knew how and he died in the place he loved. Of all the stories that can be told, this is all that matters. God rest his soul." Kiana told Lily Sir Robert had written the epitaph himself. She then took her around to some of the other larger stones and told of some of the Zantislantians. "This was my grandfather. He was a great wood carver, and loved the sea." "This was my great-great aunt. She had a beautiful voice and I heard Sir Robert loved to hear her sing." "This is the village chief from when Sir Robert was alive. They were great friends."

Lily marveled over all of these stories. She thought of how proud Grandmother Winnie would be of her coming this far. She smiled to herself as she followed Kiana back to the village.

Malosi met them and said they would like to hold a banquet in Lily's honor. Lily said she was flattered, and would like to present a gift to the village. She went back to the boat, took a much needed bath, and changed into one of her new silk shirts. She brought the rest of the bags of sugar with her, which she formally presented to the village. They said it reminded them of coconut sugar, and declared it a wonderful gift. While Malosi and some of the men roasted a pig, Lily helped Kiana and the other women bake some sweets using a bit of the sugar.

As the sun began to set, the sky turned pink, then purple with a touch of orange, and then a green flash burst forth as the sun sank into the sea. Lily marveled at it. She had never seen anything quite like it, even in Fanea. That night, the fire blazed high as they danced, ate, and talked. More stories of Sir Robert were told, as well as stories of the mighty men and women of the past. Many things reminded Lily of

Yurisvenia, but there were other things that solely belonged to Zantislan. Lily loved them both, as well as all the places she had visited. She couldn't believe how far she had come, or how much she had learned. Feeling safer here than she had in a long time, Lily went back to her ship to fall into a deep, much needed sleep.

Lily had been invited to breakfast the next morning, so she headed back to the village just as the sun was rising. There was an assortment of eggs, roasted chicken, and rice, as well as fruits Lily had never seen before. The siblings Malosi and Kiana asked Lily if they might help her repair the Robyn's Nest, as they had seen the damage when she had landed. She gratefully accepted and a large group gathered boards and various items to get the old ship into better shape. They were happy to see it, as most had only heard the legends about it. Any who had seen it were very young at the time and only had faint memories left.

Lily put her old, still rather blood stained shirt back on so she could help with the work. They took off the boards used in the quick repair, cut the broken boards, and mended the gap . When they were done, not a crack was left. Some of the skilled metal workers took a look at her furnace and told her that the patch she had done wasn't bad, but there was damage much deeper in that they couldn't repair. They told her that they could build a new furnace that should give her the lift she needed whenever she wanted to try and fly again. She readily agreed. Lily tried to pay them with some of the items she had gotten in Allegande, but they absolutely refused. The only payment they would accept was any help she could provide to the village during her stay.

Happy to help, Lily began asking around the villagers to find tasks that she might be able to perform. One elderly woman said she needed help sowing her garden. Lily thought it would be nice to learn how to grow the crops that thrived on Zantislan. Many things grew wild, but the villagers preferred cultivating some of the roots and potatoes so they were easier to find. She weeded the small patch of ground, then helped the woman plant and fertilize the rows. Lily came back week after week to check in on the plants and help weed. It was a joy watching the sprouts come up and thrive in the sun.

She also learned to spear fish. Malosi took her out with a group of younger children and showed them all how to spot the fish in the water and wait for just the right moment before bringing the spear down. Much like her trials with shooting a target, the spear fishing took patience and focus, and try as she might, Lily kept missing. She laughed in self-depreciation as Malosi came over to check on her progress.

"The 9-year-old kids seem to be excelling at this, but my aim is always off," she sighed.

Malosi laughed. "That's because you haven't lived near water. Look at the rocks at the bottom of the pool. You see how the water magnifies them? And how the sun reflects back in your eyes from the surface? You can't hunt anything underwater the same as you do on land. Nothing is quite the way it seems when looking down into the sea. You have to take that into account when launching your spear."

Seeing the sense in this, Lily practiced aiming for rocks, taking note of where her spear landed when she thought she had one dead in her sights. She began to see how the image of the spear was refracted, and how to best position it for better aiming.

After a few days of testing her throw, a large silver fish came near. Checking its distance and depth, Lily made a quick throw. The spear dove through the water, catching the fish in the side. Drawing her pole back, she saw the fish was firmly staked on the end. Turning to Malosi with a big grin, she showed him her prize. He clapped her on the back, saying "Now you've got it!"

She was pleased to roast and share her fish that evening. There is a sense of accomplishment in being able to catch your own dinner. This reminded her of the time she spent with the Elder in Avoclaide, fishing with poles and nets, and trapping small game. She hoped he was doing well, and that more villagers had come to visit.

Lily never imagined she could be this happy again. At evening gatherings, many of the children would ask her tell them the stories of the places she had seen, with Kiana helping to translate. Their favorite was the tale of the fierce cat that she had defended herself against. She would also tell them stories of her youth, and wisdom she had learned from Grandmother Winnie.

Daytimes were spent helping repair homes, build bridges over the small streams, or any other small task the villagers had for her. Sometimes she would gather fruit. Kiana taught her how to climb the big coconut trees, twisting the ripe coconuts off of the cluster, and safely dropping them down to the sand. This involved tying rope around her ankles to keep them steady, and then inching her way up the enormous trees. Lily preferred the ones that leaned to the side, telling herself that if she fell, it would at least be at a lower height than the straight ones.

After their hard work, Kiana would smash a small hole in the fruit and drain the milk into a bowl she carried. Each woman took turns sipping the sweet liquid. Then she would crack it open, take out her knife, and cut chunks out for them to enjoy.

One day, the metal workers came to ask for her assistance gathering ore for her furnace parts. They had used the rest of their store working on parts for it, and now they needed to replenish their supplies. She had never even seen a mine before, but they were doing all this work for her. All she had really done were small chores for the village as payment, so she wanted to help them in any way she could.

They brought her to a small cave opening, and handed her a lantern, a woven basket that fit on her shoulders, and a pickaxe. The men bent down to enter, and Lily followed suit. Inside, the lantern beams hit the walls, revealing reddish stones. A strong, musty odor pervaded the cavern. The men showed Lily where to place her lantern for the best light, and how to hold her pickaxe. She gave a few swings with promising results. It was hard work, but thankfully they were only gathering what they needed. By evening, they had enough loaded into their baskets to smelt into more parts for her furnace.

At twilight most evenings, Lily loved going to the beach and staring out at the calm sea that encircled the island. Rough waves were lovely and fierce, but this almost mirror-like stillness was calm and beautiful. During one of these times of reflection, Malosi and Kiana joined her and mentioned wanting to take her out to see the reefs, but Lily bashfully told them she had only swam in the small creeks that were near her home in Callingford. She wasn't sure if she would be able to swim out so far in this deep water. Kiana told her not to worry, she would teach her. They spent an afternoon in the shallower pools near the shore, Kiana using powerful strokes, and Lily following more reluctantly behind. Soon, Lily felt more comfortable, and could swim with Kiana easily. It had been a long time, but Lily remembered when Grandmother Winnie taught her to swim in the little stream by their campsite. Lily panicked at first when her feet couldn't touch the bottom, but Grandmother Winnie just held on to her and told her to relax and float. Once she got used to the feeling of weightlessness, she learned some basic strokes. These were what came back to Lily now. With Kiana's guidance, she practiced diving to the low sea floor and picking up shells. The sun began to set, so they finished their swim for the day and decided to try for the deeper areas the next day.

After a light breakfast the following morning, Malosi and Kiana took Lily back to the ocean and taught her how to use a bamboo tube to breathe through while snorkeling. They made short paddling motions with their feet and gracefully moved their bodies through the water with long, sweeping motions of their arms. They chose a place that was deeper, but closer to shore for the sake of Lily's first venture out. As she looked through the waving blue light filtering down, Lily could see bright coral plants swaying in the water. A school of striped fish swam nearby, and an eel popped out of a hole in the rock wall. With such magnificent views, Lily could see why Sir Robert loved it here so much.

After Lily had been in Zantislan for two months, she finally had an opportunity to prove herself, at least in her own eyes. Kiana came to her with a problem one evening, asking if she might have any advice. It seems they were having an issue with an unknown type of rodent that was stealing their crops. Lily thought this was odd, since they were on an island, and having anything new appear would be rather difficult. Kiana told her that there was a mountain farther away on the island, and some animals lived there that usually did not visit the village, but once every few decades, something like this would happen. Lily said she would try and help if she could.

Kiana took her to the latest "theft", where Malosi was already checking the half chewed crops as well as a hole that had been dug into a shed. "This doesn't look like the work of any of the normal animals that come around here at night. Thankfully, it only seems interested in vegetables, and not the livestock," he said.

There had already been an attempt at capturing it, but the creature had avoided the pit trap that had been set. They islanders were trying not to kill it, if possible. Lily remembered what the Elder had taught her back in Avoclaide. "Let me try something," she said.

Working all the next day, Lily took some wires that she had on the Robyn's Nest and twisted them to form a small box with an open end. She placed a wooden plate with a spring in the center, and attached this to a door that would close when even slight pressure was applied. That evening, they placed the trap by the shed and baited it with a carrot, making sure all the other vegetables were safely stored elsewhere. Everyone found a place to hide themselves far enough away to not cause alarm, but close enough to see what they would catch. In about an hour, a small, grey rat-like creature came stealthily through the yard. Smelling the carrot, it cautiously moved around the trap, sniffing the edges. Finding nothing amiss, the creature crept in toward the bait. As soon as its front feet hit the plate, the door slammed shut, startling the animal. Cheers went up, much to Lily's satisfaction. Malosi picked up the trap and said he would take it up around the mountain the next day, hoping this episode was enough to scare it off, or other measures would eventually have to be taken. It wasn't a lot, but she felt like she had been able to achieve something while she was here.

During the months of her stay, she continued to live on the Robyn's Nest, but came into the village to share food and help work every day. It was a wonderful existence, but Lily knew she wasn't ready to settle here yet. She still had so many things to see and do. Who knew how many other places Sir Robert had seen and never spoken of, or had never been to at all?

As spring approached, Lily asked the metal workers if the small ignition furnace was ready to be installed. It was time to head home for a while. She was told there were a few parts that still needed to be forged, but it could be done in a weeks time. They even asked if she would like to take part in finished some of the smaller bits. She readily agreed, always having been fascinated by blacksmithing.

She watched as they melted down and refined the ore she had helped gather. Lily helped them pour the molten iron into prepared molds, and then assisted as they filed off and polished the cooled parts. It was hot standing near the blazing furnace, but she felt rewarded seeing the finished products.

Lily made her preparations as the new furnace was being finished. All her canned food had been used by this point, so she dried fish, salted pork, and gathered fruits, vegetables, and roots to use on her way back, as well as a bag she filled with something special the day before she left. She used the river that flowed near the village to refresh her tanks and made sure her boiler was in good shape. In two weeks, she was ready to go. The extra furnace had been installed and only had to be tried.

The night before she left, Malosi and Kiana threw a huge party for her. Another pig was roasted, and Lily was glad to help provide fish, plants, and fruit for the party. Much to her surprise, Malosi and Kiana ceremonially gifted Lily a feathered hair comb, beautifully decorated with long and short plumes of green, blue, and white. She thanked them profusely, and wore it for the rest of the evening.

The whole village came down to the beach the next day to see her off. Lily hugged Malosi and Kiana, and thanked the Zantislantians for all of their help. Climbing aboard, she made sure the bag she had packed the day before was near at hand. She lit the furnaces, both balloons inflated properly, and the ship lifted into the air just as it should. Opening the bag, she began to throw handfuls of flowers down on the well wishers as she ascended. The crowd gasped and laughed, catching the blooms as they floated down. Everyone waved goodbye as she sailed off, Lily waving just as hard from above.

CHAPTER ELEVEN

The first stop on the way back would be Fanea, back on the Tartian islands. She hoped the volcano would no longer be erupting, because she knew she could easily get the canned food she needed there to replenish her supplies. She also hoped there would be guava pastries.

The way there was only open ocean, which was a little scary, but Lily felt much more confident in her new repairs, and had a better idea of where she was on the map now. She had enough food to last for about two weeks, so she wasn't doing badly there either. She just had to hope the clear skies continued.

After about 10 days, Lily began to see the islands come into view. The volcano had gone dormant again and everything seemed back to normal. She landed at the yard and immediately went to the bakery. They had added a lemon curd turnover to their offerings so Lily purchased one of these to accompany the guava puff. Then she finished the less exciting job of picking out more canned food. When these were safely stored onboard, Lily went to watch the sunset on the beach again. It amazed her that not only was every sunset different from the last, but each one was influenced by the area she was in. The sunsets here were beautiful, but none compared to the ones she had seen on Zantislan.

Lily sent one more postcard to the Applegates, wondering if it would make it back before she did. She had no idea how fast the post travelled from the islands. She only gave a brief account of some of the worst problems, not wishing to worry them too much.

The next day Lily set her ship to head back to Callingford. She estimated it was going to take her about a week and a half, so she was glad she had fresh supplies. She thought about visiting her new friends in Yurisvenia and Avoclaide. She knew it would take too much time to go back and visit Yurisvenia, and she didn't want to make the Applegates worry too much. She had only been able to send one postcard before everything had happened, and one after. She did worry about the Elder, though, so she decided to make a stop there to check on him. Lily readjusted her course, and then used the travel time to write the rest of her adventures down in her journal. She cleaned up some of her old entries and looked back over the recipes she had written. It wasn't a bad start.

Thankfully, the trip was uneventful, aside from a few sprinkles of rain that gave Lily a bit of a scare at first. At this point, Lily was over solid ground so she made a quick landing in an open space. It only lasted for an hour, and soon the sun came back from behind the clouds. She was still glad that she had chosen to be cautious.

Once back in the air and making good time, the trees of Avoclaide began to appear on her right. She found the glade where she had landed before and made her way down. It was still light out, so Lily made her way into the trees, calling "hellos" before her, so as not to scare the Elder or anyone else who might be there. Making her way through the trees, her calls were soon returned by a familiar voice. Coming to the camp, Lily found the Elder sitting by his fire, waving as she came into sight.

"Well met, old friend," he said as she took his hand.

"Hello, Elder. How are you? Are you still getting visitors up here?"

The Elder gestured to the trees, pointing out stairs that Lily had failed to see on her way in, having only been focused on her friend. "I even have a few new residents. They don't come out much during the day, but they are making headway there. They have decided to try living in the trees again. My old bones can't make it up the stairs easily, though, so I stay down here. I went up once, when they first started building, but they had to help me back down. It was still a wonderful experience to be back up among the leaves again."

"I'm glad of that. Is there anything I can do while I'm here?"

The Elder shook his head. "I have everything I need. I would love to hear of your travels, though, if you're willing to stay and talk"

Lily was happy to speak with him, and they spent the rest of the day talking about the things Lily had seen since she left. As the sun began to set, the other villagers came out of their homes. There were about eight of them now, five men and three women. They were surprised to see Lily again, but welcomed her. The Elder told them some of her stories, and he translated for one of the men.

"We thought you were foolish, speaking of trees and wind. Now we see that it is good above ground as well. Now we can move about more freely. There are still many who are too scared to come up, and are content to live only below. We have all decided that each man will do what he likes, and will not force the others to do what they do not want to do."

Lily thought this sounded like a good plan. After all, it's no good forcing people to do things against their will.

She stayed on three more days, speaking with the new villagers and helping the Elder with small chores. He was well taken care of, as the others made sure he had everything he needed. Lily was glad she didn't have to worry about her friend anymore. He could live his life out the way he wanted.

Saying her goodbyes once again, and promising to come back anytime she was in the area, she set her sights back for home.

It was early morning when she left, and she figured it would be about 9 hours before she finished her trip. She added to her journal and cleared up her pantry, then sat down to enjoy her records. In the late afternoon, the tall, brick buildings of Callingford appeared over the horizon and made Lily realize how homesick she had been. She loved seeing the world, but she had been gone for almost a year. There may be nothing exciting here, but it was her home. All of her memories with Grandmother Winnie flooded in on her, but she was glad to remember them. Much of the sting had been removed from them.

Lily landed at the shipyard and made her way straight to the Applegate's home. She used the knocker, and both Collin and Hannah appeared at the door, with Duchess at their ankles. They were overjoyed to see her and practically drug her into the house. They had just received her last note that morning, and were presently discussing it. Over tea, Lily gave them the full tale. They sat in wonder over the large eyed children, gasped when she told them about the volcano, smiled when she told of Yurisvenia, were terrified when she explained how she shot the big cat, and were thrilled that she had found Zantislan. She apologized for not sending more letters, but most of the places she had stopped at did not have the ability. She was afraid she had worried them.

"We just prayed for a safe return and hoped you were doing everything you dreamed of," Collin said. "That's all we can do for others when they are away."

Hannah said "We're glad you're back for a bit and safe now. Your room is all ready for you, so please feel free to stay." Lily was grateful for this. She still had nowhere else to go.

She also knew that she would have to start to make some money on her own for a while before her next trip. That night at dinner, Lily asked Collin and Hannah what they thought she might be able to do.

"Have you ever thought about doing a speaking tour? People usually enjoy hearing stories about faraway places. I still happen to know quite a few people from the circus that still manage things like that," Hannah replied.

Was there nothing the Applegates couldn't do? "That would be perfect! I'm not sure how well I would do speaking in front of a crowd, but I will certainly do my best."

The next few weeks were spent paying calls to Hannah's friends, mailing flyers, and making arrangements for gathering halls and schools in the surrounding area. The flyers read "Come hear the great explorer Lily Fairfax regale you with tales of her latest adventures." Lily thought this was a bit much, but Hannah assured her it was necessary in order to drum up the excitement. Her first presentation was scheduled for the local town hall where all but ten of the tickets had already been sold. Lily hoped she wouldn't disappoint the crowd. Collin and Hannah had let her practice for them and they seemed to think she was ready.

The evening of the talk, Lily paced back and forth behind the stage, waiting for the announcer to introduce her. She heard her name being called, and she timidly stepped out from behind the curtain. A sea of faces greeted her, which made her stop in her tracks for a moment. This was almost worse than being chased by the big cat. That thought made her laugh to herself, which helped calm her down. She walked up to the mike and said "Hello, I'm Lily. My adventure began when I made the dubious purchase of the famous Robyn's Nest. Long before that, though, I had been raised on the stories of Sir Robert Pettigrew. Let me tell you a little about my Grandmother Winnie..."

Front Cover Photo By Sherry Cooke